FLAME

Saripalli Venkata Ravi Kiran

INDIA • SINGAPORE • MALAYSIA

A souvenir to Smt. Sujatha, my wife, who prompted me to write a love story!

Thanks to Namita who designed an exceptional cover page!

Thanks to Sri Voleti Srinivasa Bhanu Garu who guided me. As a seasoned writer, columnist and poet, he possessed a remarkable understanding of the lives, emotions and journeys of all sections of society, as is evident from his must-read literature books- Belgaum Kathalu and Pogabandi Kathalu. It is a privilege to learn from him who has honed his craft to such a high level of expertise.

Thanks to NVSS Somayajulu, my friend, who hinted at subtle tips and those nuances helped enhance my imagination.

Thanks to Sailesh and Alekya for concurrent editing.

Thanks to Sri Durga Chaudhary for invaluable inputs.

Contents

1. Bet Was On 7
2. She Put the Finger on Her Own Dad.................25
3. He Resolved to Deepdive 39
4. Drama at the Downstream Riverbed.................55
5. Journey to Hyderabad not Without Hitches 71
6. A Clue That Eluded a Breakthrough 87
7. Suryam Hit the Bullseye...............................101
8. Love Conquered All 111

CHAPTER 1

Bet Was On

Sea breeze was gently passing through the corridors of Barrackpore cantonment, West Bengal.

Emotionally choked 49-year-old Havildar Padem Veeraiah stood in attention. After two decades of immaculate service, it was the day for him to superannuate from service. A company of senior sepoys assembled to bid him farewell.

Two days ago, Veeraiah, during patrolling duty, spotted sightings of questionable movement on the India-Bangladesh border.

Brigadier Antony Stelins glanced at Veeraiah appreciatively. He walked to the podium and remarked, "Veeraiah has set the highest standards. His unwavering dedication is exemplified by his fearless patrolling of the borders. I wish him a happy and healthy retirement."

Veeraiah reciprocated, "Sir, I thank the Almighty, my Unit, my wife and my daughter who stood by me through thick and thin."

* * *

Three days later, when Veeraiah reached Bhadrachalam, his hometown in Telangana state, and stepped into his house, a warm reception awaited him from his wife and daughter.

Madhavi, his 20-year-old blind daughter, affectionately handed him a greeting card. It read, *"Dearest Uncle, Wish you a peaceful and healthy retirement. Yours-Suryam!"* Suryam was the nephew of Veeraiah.

In his nephew's memory, Veeraiah felt apologetic. *'I didn't help him to join the MBBS course. He condoned me and sent me a greeting card on the eve of my retirement.'*

Madhavi preserved the greeting card preciously. Veeraiah was filled with a profound sense of tenderness towards his daughter. She lost sight in a fireworks accident during a Diwali festival.

PROJECT TIGER - MISSION 2022

Propelled by motor, three pneumatic boats were racing across the Indravati river. There were six people in each boat.

A fortnight ago, the Union Minister for Environment, Forest and Climate Change announced, "'Project Tiger 2022' will revive the Indravati Tiger Reserve. The habitat had hitherto been identified as a Maoist insurgent area. Efforts to relocate the tribals and neutralise the presence of Maoists will be stepped up. It's time to build eco-tourism."

The Mission constituted eight rangers from the Forest Department, nine sepoys and one Major from the Indian army. Of the nine sepoys chosen, 25-year-old Thotalli Suryanarayana, fondly known as Suryam, had been specially trained in soft skills. He was positioned to engage with the tribals.

A makeup to alter the features of Suryam was thought of to portray him as a forest guard! Local tribes often trusted lower grade government staff.

The pneumatic boats were racing across the river.

One sepoy displayed a photo and chuckled. Suryam promptly identified the person and said, "She is Mother Teresa!" The photo was passed to others. "Mother Teresa," everyone echoed.

"Major did the makeup. He transformed me into Mother Teresa," the sepoy giggled.

Everyone fixated their attention on Major Ravindra, Commanding Officer of the Mission. Ravindra took a pause while applying makeup on Suryam and said, "Yes. I transformed him into Mother Teresa for the fancy dress competition and he won the award for the best costume!"

Drama, theatre and makeup were Ravindra's other pursuits. All that was used by him to portray a sepoy as Mother Teresa was a white saree with a thin blue border, liquid prosthetics, wrinkled forehead and a pair of eye bags! He frequently helped the Defence Intelligence Agency make unusual facial changes on "classified officers" before they went undercover in enemy territories.

* * *

Ravindra had finished doing touch-up work on Suryam. Suryam was looking like a middle-aged forest guard!

The three boats touched the river bank of the first tribal hamlet. The leader of the hamlet received the Unit with abundant courtesies. It was unclear when the situation may escalate! Last month, Maoist Battalion Commander Saadhu was killed by the military commandos. Maoists may counter attack. The Unit was cautious of the wolf in sheep's clothing.

* * *

In Phase-I, a four-week camp was planned.

Day 1 to 4

Immediately, makeshift army tents were erected, communication radio networks and battery backups were established, while food, water, medicines and fuel were stored. Ammunition was kept handy!

Every morning, forest rangers left the hamlet tracking tiger droppings and pugmarks. Sepoys provided protection to them.

Suryam, impersonated as a forest guard, had walked around in disguise and ushered in a dialogue with the local tribals.

A sepoy was stationed managing the radio and walkie-talkie systems under the supervision of Ravindra.

Day 5 to 10

The Unit reached the third hamlet. They hardly slept. Tiger census was being conducted round the clock and it was gruellingly hard work!

Suryam managed to strike a chord with the tribals. The local tribes inhabited the core area of the National Park, intervening in the tiger's natural biosphere. He educated them about why the big cat was to be treasured. The toughest challenge was to convince the tribals to relocate.

Day 11 to 20

A significant headway was made in conducting the tiger census. There were 45 tigers! The Unit was elated. Another palpably heart-warming scenario witnessed was the dwindling count of Maoists due to the consistent weeding out operations by the military commandos.

It was 7 p.m.

The Unit gathered at the campfire outside Ravindra's tent. A sort of convivial mood set in when one ranger impromptu announced the news of his betrothal with his girlfriend! Ravindra cheered him; the topic piqued his curiosity; he had plans to meet a girl for his own marriage alliance. He lost confidence in love relationships after his girlfriend broke up with him. He was deeply in love with a beautiful woman, but unfortunately, she received a proposal from someone who was wealthier than him. She broke up and called it quits with him. He felt a range of emotions including betrayal, sadness and hurt. In fact, it was Ravindra's father who played a key role in pushing for the cancellation of his proposal to marry her. His father managed to break off the proposal as he had found a more financially well-off family.

Ravindra threw his arms into the air seeking to draw everyone's attention and announced, "Well, guys! Let me know if there're any exceptions to what I believe in! A man will love to fall in love only with a beautiful woman and a woman will love to fall in love only with a wealthy man!"

He encouraged his team to reveal their personal stories!

* * *

It was 9.30 p.m. Ravindra sat alone outside his tent. The illumination outside the tent was quite faint. On the ground, he noticed a photo of an elegant woman. It was the photo that his father sent him for his marriage alliance. *'She was breathtakingly beautiful,'* he complimented. He picked it up and was about to place it back in the purse. But her photo remained intact in his purse! He was surprised.

He saw Suryam walking briskly enquiring his fellow sepoys about something.

"Sir! Have you found a photo of a female?" Suryam asked as he reached Ravindra.

"Is this one?" Ravindra displayed it.

"Yes, Sir!" Suryam's face gladdened.

"What is she to you?" Ravindra enquired as he handed the photo to Suryam.

"Sir! She is **KIRTANA. SHE** is my everything. **SHE** completes me. She was the one I talked about when we all met at the campfire here!" replied Suryam as he carefully secured the photo in its slot in the purse!

* * *

Ravindra shifted uneasily on the bed. It was midnight. Suryam's narration about Kirtana was reverberating inside his mind. A symphony of claps admiring Suryam's love story erupted at the campfire and it was unsettling Ravindra!

Suryam said he was from a low caste and poor family background. She hailed from an upper caste and was affluent. He followed her like an ordinary fan of a star heroine. He was good at studies and drawing and she admired him. He was about to join as a gatekeeper at a movie theatre, and she persuaded him to write the NEET test. He got top rank and admission into an MBBS course at CMC, Vellore. Due to inexplicable reasons, he decided to join the army. He had no courage to inform her. He texted her an SMS that he joined the army as sepoy and pleaded with her to forgive him and forget him. She replied back:

'YOU MAY BECOME A DOCTOR OR DRIVER OF A TRACTOR OR A SOLDIER. IT MATTERS LITTLE TO ME ABOUT WHAT YOU ARE! WE LIVE FOR EACH OTHER AND ONE DAY WE SHALL GET MARRIED!"

It was 1 a.m. Ravindra tossed uncomfortably on the bed. He was determined to tie the knot with Kirtana and didn't want to let her slip through his fingers. He loved a beautiful woman but she broke up with him and married a man wealthier than him. He lost confidence in love. Arranged marriage is the norm in his family. His father had an arranged marriage. His mother descended like a Goddess of wealth in his father's life. His dad said an arranged marriage was a means to multiply net-worth. Kirtana hailed from Paloncha which was a hundred kilometres from his native town, Khammam. His father sent him her photo. She looked like an angel. He was a Major in the army and was proud of his physique. His father and her father were landlords and belonged to the same caste. Astrologers cleared the proposal. They would make a perfect match, he assessed. But, alas! He had not anticipated the twist in the tale. He became aware that Suryam and Kirtana were in a relationship. It was an impractical alliance, he cursed. He would meet and impress her and rest would fall in place, 25-year-old Ravindra resolved. The challenge sounded sweet and lulled him into sleep!

Day 21 to 28

Recce of the count of live tigers had come to an end. The rangers had set up cameras to capture stripe patterns of tigers. It was decided they would soon return to the Reserve for a review. Tribals were yet showing resistance to relocate. The Unit sensed a quiet influence by Maoists.

Last day of the camp: 10 a.m.

Ravindra addressed the Unit before they dispersed, "I congratulate on successfully conducting the tiger census. Suryam shall lead the proceedings till you reach Raipur. I'm going on a different mission. I shall be picked up in an hour or two from here. Good luck!"

The seventeen-member Unit carried the backpack and walked down to the river bank.

Ravindra readied to contact the headquarters and submit a summary of the outcome of the camp. At that moment, he noticed a radio signal. He heard an incoming message.

"This is Headquarters. Intel, over!"

Ravindra responded, "This is Reserve 202. I'm alone. Roger! Over!"

"Detain sepoy Suryanarayana................................... Roger! Over!" It was a long message.

"Roger, over," Ravindra closed the call.

He was stunned to know the reason to detain Suryam. He immediately contacted him on walkie talkie and instructed, "Suryam! You return and report to me. Except you, rest all to go ahead! Over!"

Suryam complied, "Yes Sir. Roger, over!" Ravindra could not understand Suryam's unclear and feeble response. He said, "Suryam! Your message is coming in broken. Please say it again! Over!" Suryam repeated his message. Once more, due to signal issues, the message was broken. Ravindra had no time. It was an instruction to him from the Intelligence Services to detain Suryam! He hung the gun and a bag with cartridges over his shoulder and sprinted down the slope toward the river bank.

Ravindra's thoughts raced ahead of him. Was Suryam framed? Suryam could not have done this crime, he believed. Ravindra witnessed Suryam's bravery and selfless commitment. Fitness was the cornerstone of a soldier's readiness and resilience and Suryam was above par in his Unit. Suryam was a marvel in stamina and endurance. He lived by a strict code of ethics. His perseverance and never-say-die attitude in the face of challenges made a formidable force to reckon with. His critical thinking and attention to detail were highly valued by Ravindra himself. Last year, Suryam demonstrated immense courage by risking his life to save soldiers who were under siege by five terrorists. He disguised himself as a media person, used his skills to approach the terrorists and killed them, ultimately leading to the successful rescue of the soldiers.

Should he go by the instructions of the headquarters and arrest him or not arrest an honest soldier! If he decided not to arrest Suryam, what reason should he cite to his headquarters? He found himself facing a difficult situation, a moral dilemma! He reached the river bank. The pneumatic boats already moved from the bank with the Unit on board. Ravindra was about to scream to draw their attention. He heard gunfire. He hid behind a tree and studied the surroundings.

The sepoys seemed to have heard gunshots and they began to retaliate. Suddenly, there were a series of deafeningly huge explosions on the river. Next moment, Ravindra was shell-shocked to witness a ghastly scene. The boats were hit by explosions and bodies blew into the air. Bodies of the rangers and the sepoys were strewn all over the river. Hiding behind marshy swamps, Maoists were firing indiscriminately.

Bullets randomly flew in the direction of Ravindra's hide! Someone grasped Ravindra and thrusted him to the ground in a flash at the nick of the moment. Ravindra looked at the person who shoved him. It was Suryam! Both lay flat on their stomachs and crawled to safety, seeking refuge behind a sturdy banyan tree.

Suryam and Ravindra took to counter attack. Maoists faced a fierce volley of bullets. Two Maoists were killed before the rest fled the scene.

Ravindra and Suryam immediately jumped into the river in search of survivors. There were no survivors! Both swam back and sat at the bank. They were speechless. Tall Sal and Teak trees stood in mourning. Mutilated body parts were swirling in whirlpools on the Indravati River. Death was whistling and dancing!

Ravindra was mindful that Suryam rescued him from the bullets fired by Maoists. He didn't notice the bullets being fired in his direction till Suryam thrusted him just in time. But he didn't express his appreciation.

Meanwhile, Suryam thanked wiping his moist eyes, "Sir, you saved me. I was about to step onto the boat before you instructed me to report back."

Ravindra felt he was not sure whether he saved Suryam or whether he was going to make it tougher for him. His mind was working in overdrive to hatch an idea! Would not a capable and intelligent Suryam, when he was not arrested, lend crucial aid in his next mission to capture the criminals of the currency mafia, Ravindra pondered.

He saw a signal on the radio. He knew it was from Headquarters seeking confirmation about the detention of Suryam. He decided to lie. His heart was pounding. He made up his mind! He sighed deeply and snorted out an exhale.

He responded on the mobile radio. "This is Reserve 202. Roger, over!"

"This is Headquarters. Report in. Over!"

Ravindra gave an empty stare at Suryam as he replied to Headquarters, "Reserve 202. Sad news. The entire Unit of Project Tiger 2022, including Suryanarayana, died. Maoists ambushed us. Two Maoists were killed. Please depute a rescue team. Over."

Suryam looked puzzled. He was left in a state of confusion and shock when Ravindra confirmed to the Headquarters that Suryam had also perished.

"Suryam," Ravindra explained, "I've received an instruction to take you into custody. Our Intelligence Services found two lakhs worth Rs.2000 fake currency notes in an envelope received in your name by post. Two more soldiers from your hometown were also charged with the same crime and they were taken into custody."

Suryam was stunned to know the charges levelled against him. He was shocked to know the names of the other two sepoys who were already detained. They were his bosom friends, classmates at the school and were dedicated soldiers!

"Who dispatched fake currency?" Suryam asked in a faint voice.

"That's what is to be detected now! Seems to be the work of the mafia, Suryam!" Ravindra spelt out, "Fake currency is being smuggled through porous international borders and is reaching Hyderabad. It's suspected that someone from the army is hand in glove. I'm assigned to investigate the matter.

"I've to report to the Regional Centre, Hyderabad from here. You join me in my next mission. I don't want to arrest you. You will be my 'ghost' assistant from now on. You are dead for the world. I want you to operate incognito.

"In case I detain you, you too will languish in jails. The Headquarters may treat the case as closed. The real criminal shall continue the crime unabated. Such a situation must not persist. We must capture the perpetrator and rid the nation of any traitors. After the mission is over, I will announce to the world that you are alive and that you have assisted me. It's my call!"

Fixing the real criminal was his default priority and Suryam was crucial to pursue it. However, Ravindra right away and instantly became aware of another potential possibility. Suddenly, he experienced a light bulb moment. When Kirtana had become aware of Suryam's death and when he was not present in her life, it might erase the fleeting affection and adolescent infatuation she might have had towards Suryam and Ravindra's fresh entry into her life would pave a way to marry her, Ravindra schemed.

Suryam was listening wide eyed. His supervisor had given him a clean chit. Ravindra decided not to hand him to the army police. Moreover, Ravindra made him part of his vital mission.

Suryam felt overwhelmed by the trust and confidence that Ravindra reposed in him. He resolved to go to any lengths to serve his boss and the country. He was convinced to die a fake death and operate incognito.

He was dead for his mother! Could she bear the loss, he measured. Well, she experienced many heart-wrenching losses, he thought.

He was dead for……. KIRTANA! Suddenly, he felt agony. *'Kirtana cannot bear the news of my death.'*

Ravindra didn't even wait for Suryam's response. He knew for sure Suryam would comply with his instruction.

"Suryam," Ravindra commanded as he strolled ahead, "you leave for Paloncha now. I've to be part of the retrieval operations of the dead bodies. We shall meet in Paloncha next week. Move in disguise and hide your identity. Follow my makeup tips. Modify your accent and tone."

There was no reply from Suryam. Ravindra looked behind and observed Suryam's face growing stoic. He heard Suryam muttering in a lower tone, "Sir, Kirtana may not survive the news of my death! I may not die a fake death."

Ravindra had not anticipated that Suryam would negate his order! Blood surged through his nerves. He gnawed his teeth angrily, mocked and repeated the words uttered by Suryam, *'Sir, Kirtana may not survive the news of my death!'*

He castigated, "So, shall we leave the real offender go scot-free? Why may Kirtana not survive your death? Nonsense!" He rejected the idea of LOVE. "Suryam, Kirtana showed compassion for you. Compassion for the poor! Mercy for her poor school friend! Don't get emotional! When it comes to love or whatever nonsense you name it, she will choose a man from a wealthy family!"

Unable to digest the tide of tirade unleashed by Ravindra ridiculing the relationship between him and Kirtana, Suryam seethed with frustration. Frustration led to anger.

He reiterated stubbornly, "Kirtana cannot bear the news of my death!"

"Is she in blind love with you?" a string of satirical laugh was heard.

"Don't make fun of our love!" a strand of warning resonated in Suryam's voice!

"Well, Suryam," Ravindra said, raising his voice, "at least it's not fun to say we are in the 21st century. Break ups among lovers, like trendy cars, are racing along fast lanes! Love is a multi-layered feeling. It's love for beauty, skin, money, cushy jobs, luxurious cars, lavish travel, land, villas, bank balance and fame! These aspects will determine the quotient of love!"

"Stop degrading our love!" Suryam warned.

"It's my bet. Kirtana will forget you in no time! She will move on! Your death is a non-event for her. I bet she will marry someone matching her profile! You mistook her compassion for you as love," Ravindra confronted.

Suryam disagreed. He revolted. "She will never forget me! She will not marry anyone else!" he shouted.

An animated debate erupted between the two; a passionate argument exploded; a serious quarrel escalated. Ravindra found the insubordination of Suryam intolerable. He cautioned Suryam.

Suryam had not capitulated. Ravindra had not relented. Suryam had boundless faith in the sincerity of Kirtana's love, while Ravindra had immeasurable conviction that social status and wealth would play a predominant role for a girl to select her life partner!

A stalemate calcified.

The two betted! They signed a written agreement. Both signed and exchanged the 'bet' agreement copies between them.

The agreement set the rules. Suryam should move in disguise! He should not reveal his identity to Kirtana or anyone till Ravindra gave him the green signal. If Suryam's identity is revealed to her or anyone, he should walk out of her life. If Suryam discovered that she had chosen to marry someone else, he should respectfully remove himself from her life. The responsibility to maintain secrecy of identity solely lies with Suryam. He should pursue investigation and assist Ravindra nab the criminal etc, etc.

Cogent rules were drafted and signed off!

Suryam took a copy of the agreement. He vowed that he would participate in Ravindra's mission, capture the criminals, exonerate himself and his two friends of the accusation and secure their release from imprisonment. He swore that he would prove to Ravindra that Kirtana's love for him was spotless and was as pure as flame!

Ravindra secured the agreement copy. He resolved he should take utmost care that at no point Suryam should grasp that he was scheming to marry Kirtana!

CHAPTER 2

She Put the Finger on Her Own Dad

"She's on the first floor," said Saguleti Nagabhushanam, Kirtana's father.

"Has she had her breakfast?" Ravindra enquired as he walked toward the wooden staircase with shopping paper bags in his hands.

"This morning," Nagabhushanam replied, "she consumed lemon juice."

Ravindra smiled and said, "Uncle, soon she will be normal. My parents have bought a diamond necklace and silk sarees for her. Let me cheer her up."

Nagabhushanam tried to escort him. Ravindra gently stopped him and said, "Well, that's okay uncle! I'm familiar with your house. This is my third visit!"

* * *

Ravindra paced up and down the room for a couple of times before he sat opposite Kirtana on a chair.

Kirtana sat dejectedly on the sofa and was staring at the floor.

"My parents are excited. They're planning to visit you soon. They sent you a necklace," With a smile on his face, he paraded the gifts he had bought for her. She didn't look at him nor at the gifts. Plunged in desolation, she was feeling drained! The news of the death of Suryam that she heard on the television crushed her.

Unmindful of her agony, Ravindra's parents, her parents and Ravindra were pursuing the marriage alliance. During the first meeting, she politely conveyed to Ravindra her lack of interest in marriage!

"Well," Ravindra had a readymade answer to assuage, "it's hard to get along when a friend passes away. I understand your sadness! Army too lost brave sepoys! I'm equally sad! Life should go on. Please count on me to help you revive!"

Icy silence reigned.

"SURYAM is not just a friend! HE is my life! You leave me alone!" Kirtana felt like screaming.

She saw him walking up to the window.

"Spacious garden! Nice bungalow! Your dad seems like a good planner. He built his home away from his rice mill. How serene it's here!" Ravindra spoke randomly appreciating the expansive bungalow. He side-glanced at the poster of Suryam pasted on the wall! *Puppy love. Immature feelings'* he shook his head in total disappointment.

"I'm not interested in marriage!" her choked throat spluttered. He heard her very distinctly and underwent an involuntary spasm in his stomach. Disregarding the pain and the embarrassment, he babbled irrelevantly, "Kirtana, you've a wonderful taste. It's a lovely flower garden."

He stepped toward the doorway of her bedroom. He consoled himself that she merely said she was not interested in marriage. More often than not women made such subjective statements. It was not to be taken as a refusal of him. He decided to revisit her with more expensive gifts. He knew her preference for white colour and he made a decision to purchase a pearls necklace for her. Yet, he felt insecure and to generate some amount of goodwill, he blurted, "Kirtana, I thank the Almighty for sparing you as my partner! I pray for you to give you strength in this hour of grief! See you tomorrow!"

Kirtana's blue eyeballs shifted in his direction and feeling relief, her eyes saw him off!

Ravindra came down the staircase. Nagabhushanam and his wife were tensely waiting for him. Ravindra showed thumbs up and said, "Uncle, she took the necklace. She bid me a warm farewell!"

* * *

Ravindra was driving back to Khammam in Grand Vitara. *"What a graceful lady! Her blue eyes are like glistening droplets that adorn grass flowers in the early mornings during the winter. Her grief-stricken soft face is like a silver moon frosted by a thin layer of clouds! Her lips are like soft petals of red roses! I cannot wait to win her heart!"* he reckoned in anguish.

Suddenly, the memory of Suryam interrupted his train of thought. Where he was, Ravindra felt anxious. Suryam's whereabouts were not known, he had no phone as he was restricted from using one, he had no KYC document and he was like a fugitive leading a life incognito.

Ravindra himself burnt the KYC documents of Suryam in his presence except the name badge on his uniform! He took it and preserved it with him. He was keen they should meet before the casket carrying his 'mortal remains' reached Paloncha!

It took four days for recovery of the bodies from the Indravati river. The bodies of the sepoys and rangers were beyond recognition. The DNA specialists adopted a forensic process to complete the autopsy. A name badge with surname 'Thotalli' was found by the search team at the blast site. 'Thotalli' was Suryam's surname! Ravindra camped at the 'blast site' till seventeen caskets were sealed and readied for despatch. When the seventeenth casket was sealed, one of the specialists said, "It's a complex random identification process beyond simple visual recognition. Thank you, Ravindra, for your support."

* * *

Four days ago-

The government passenger bus halted at Bhadrachalam bus station. After a tedious journey from Indravati National Park via Bastar latching onto multiple modes of road transport, Suryam sighed with relief when he knew it was another one hour before he stepped on the soil of Paloncha, his hometown.

Suryam spotted a television inside a sweet vending shop. A flashy Telugu serial was being telecast. He carefully read the news being scrolled at the bottom of the screen. No news about Maoists encounter was being streamed. *'It seems the news is not yet announced!'* he speculated.

He was about to board the bus. He saw his parents! His mother was wailing and rushing out of the bus station. His father, a dipsomaniac, was as usual in a drunken state and was ambling behind his wife in a disconcerted way.

Suryam was dismayed.

He followed his parents in disguise.

The auto-rickshaw dropped his parents at his maternal uncle-Padem Veeraiah's residence. Suryam witnessed his mother in a state of inconsolable sobbing. He noticed a shamiyana in front of the house. Neighbours assembled. He walked on the sideways and observed a dead body placed under the shamiyana. He was shocked. It was the dead body of Padem Veeraiah! Soon, he learnt that his maternal uncle died in a road accident!

* * *

Veeraiah's body was cremated in the evening. Suryam paid tribute to his uncle by actively participating in the funeral rites. He introduced himself as a friend of Veeraiah. He gave Rs.50000 to his aunt and advised her to consider it as repayment of the hand loan he took from Veeraiah. His mother was grieving for her brother! His blind cousin, Madhavi, sat in a corner and was wailing.

Next day, the news of Suryam's death flashed on the TV. His mother became unconscious and was shifted to hospital. Suryam took care of his mother by staying at the hospital as her attendant. He worried his mother might identify him. He recalled one of the rules of the bet agreement signed between him and Ravindra: **THE RESPONSIBILITY TO MAINTAIN SECRECY OF IDENTITY SOLELY LIES WITH SURYAM!**

Madhavi had crestfallen at hearing the death of her cousin. Suryam overheard her saying, "Dad had a special liking for Suryam. My dad mentioned it in his diary!" She took her mother's support, opened a page in the diary and showed it to one of the relatives.

Suryam was able to gain access to the diary. Tears rolled down his cheeks as he read his uncle's handwriting, "*I didn't help Suryam to join the MBBS course. He condoned me and sent me a greeting card on the eve of my retirement.*'

He was moved to see the greeting card he had sent, carefully kept inside the diary.

* * *

Three days later-

11 a.m. It was bright and hot. Army vehicle carrying the casket of Suryam was stranded on the highway. It was gheraoed. It was not allowed to enter the town of Paloncha.

Since the sad news of Suryam's death and the spread of allegations that he was involved in currency smuggling, placards sprouted in Paloncha. Retired army personnel, students from the archery school and Suryam's college and activists of the Backward Castes (BC) community agitated demonstrating placards like "Suryam is a dedicated sepoy" 'Declare Suryam as innocent' and 'Suryam is NOT Guilty'!!

The initial mild protests had turned violent. In an act of arson, properties and vehicles of the government were set on fire. It was a spontaneous reaction by the firebrand cadre of the BC community when they listened to the latest decision of the Government: "*It has been decided to hand the casket containing the mortal remains of Suryanarayana to the members of the family **without State honours!**'*

The news that his body cremation would not be given 'state honours' angered the activists. The gherao gained massive support when none other than Kirtana herself joined the campaign. She sat in the front row of the agitation on the highway. She was flanked by a 50-year-old maths teacher, her mentor and an NGO leader. The leader of the BC community spearheaded the slogans. Kirtana veiled her face with her saree. She was crying inconsolably as shouts and slogans from hundreds of youths were booming in the air. Slogans like "We want full state honours to Suryam" "Suryam is innocent" rented the air. It was being telecast 'live' by TV news channels.

Army police and the civil police cordoned the area.

"Let's invoke the lathi *charge*," the civil police suggested. "It's your call!" the army police insisted. "Not the right time to debate technicalities; let's do it together," a senior took the initiative.

Ravindra and Suryam stood aside the army vehicle. Ravindra was pleased at Suryam's makeup. Suryam was made up to look like a middle-aged family man and was clad in mufti dress.

Suryam was growing tense when the threat of *lathi charge* loomed imminent.

The first hit of a baton fell on the NGO leader! Next to him was Kirtana! Suryam stepped forward to rescue Kirtana from the brutal hit of a *Lathi*! He even considered declaring he was alive! He stepped forward. Halfway through, he hit the brakes. Better sense prevailed! His memory evoked a rule in the agreement:

'IN CASE SURYAM VIOLATES THE AGREEMENT/ DIVULGES HIS IDENTITY WITHOUT THE CONSENT OF MAJOR RAVINDRA.........SURYAM IS TO WALK OUT OF THE LIFE OF KIRTANA FOREVER!'

Suryam saw the maths teacher escorting Kirtana to safety.

At the invocation of *lathi charge*, an unruly wave of rebellion erupted on the streets. It became free for all! The protestors outnumbered and overpowered the police. The civil police and the army police took position behind the iron barricades. Teargas shells and water cannons were fired to disperse the crowds.

The casket purportedly containing the 'mortal remains' of Suryam was moved to the Government hospital mortuary.

Kirtana was seen leaving the place along with the maths teacher in her SUV! Ravindra noticed a shade of worry on the face of Suryam. He observed that Suryam didn't bother to reveal his identity and breach the bet agreement in case Kirtana was in need of help! He overheard Suryam muttering a while ago, *'If required, I will disclose to Kirtana that I'm alive!'*

Ravindra sensed that Suryam violating the bet agreement was certain when he was in her proximity. Nowhere in the agreement was it written that Suryam should appear before Kirtana everyday! Ravindra was worried that he had missed a crucial point.

* * *

Section 144 was clamped!

A proposal was jointly mooted by the civil and the army police to take Kirtana, the maths teacher, the NGO Leader and the leader of the BCs into custody! Ravindra was part of the crucial meeting!

* * *

Ravindra was driving at a brisk pace to meet Kirtana and counsel her. He had the insider information that she would be arrested soon. Kirtana joined the street protests and the media had begun to suspect a 'romantic angle' between Suryam and Kirtana. She should stay away from the agitation, he wished. Else, the police might arrest her. His parents might drop the alliance, he worried. He was determined to explore every possible avenue and do everything to make their marriage a reality.

At the staircase, he didn't pause and peep into the office room of Nagabhushanam. He knew his prospective father-in-law had gone to consult the family astrologer.

Ravindra tiptoed the wooden staircase steps. He looked at himself, straightened his shirt collar, inhaled in a fresh breath and stepped into her room.

He saw a dejected Kirtana sitting at the study table. He glanced at the direction she was staring at! He ended up sighting the poster of Suryam on the wall! He concealed his disappointment. He placed the white pearls jewellery set at the dressing table.

As usual, he paced up and down the room. He commenced in a supplicating tone, "Kirtana, stay away from the agitation, please."

"..........."

"You will be arrested," he warned her impatiently.

He noticed she was about to say something.

"Suryam frequently spoke of your bravery. I will seek your help if need be. I want the world to leave me alone!" she said as her voice sounded hoarse due to constant wailing.

Ravindra felt abashed. He felt she was slipping away from him. He thought he should not shy away from expressing himself. He realised that a male, whether he was a Major in the army or a clerk in a government office, had to have in him a distinct ingenious dare while expressing himself to a beautiful lady.

"Well, Kirtana! Let me be clear. You will be arrested soon by the police. The agitation will die down naturally and the casket shall be handed to Suryam's family. The government may carry on a superficial investigation or even may drop it. The actual culprit of the currency mafia escapes punishment. The blemish on Suryam shall remain forever!" Ravindra paused and glanced at her.

She crossed her arms across her chest and was listening to him intensely. Her eyes continued to stare at the floor.

"Kirtana, my parents surely do not want you to go behind bars. It's a matter of social reputation. Don't squander your life participating in street protests defending a shallow feeling called love. Marry me. We would make an enviable couple. I promise you I will bring the criminal to the book. I will ensure Suryam is absolved of the allegation. I will do this for you." Ravindra thought he was reasonably eloquent.

"I can apprehend the criminal. I don't require your support!" Kirtana dug her heels in.

Ravindra felt a rude shock. He felt cornered and was annoyed.

"If you fail…...?" He questioned with a tone of disdain.

"If you fail……?" She retorted with equal vehemence.

"If I fail to catch the culprit, I will not show you my face ever after! If I succeed, we shall tie the knot," Ravindra threw the gauntlet.

"…………"

"It's the deal!" Ravindra declared.

"…………"

Ravindra displayed a harmonious smile covering up a condescending sneer. He was pleased and said in an amiable voice, "Kirtana, inform the media that you're out of the agitation to avoid being arrested."

"We've taken anticipatory bail," she gave a cold reply.

"That's great! Time to start my investigation," a buoyant Ravindra assured her and left.

She saw his face awash with a sense of victory!

Tearfully she brooded: *'Ravindra, I'm sure I will **not** let you win! I will **not** let you tie the knot! I'm sure to win! Because, I already know who the criminal is. **It's my father!'***

CHAPTER 3

He Resolved to Deepdive

The news of the likely arrest of Kirtana and others which was supposed to stay confidential sneaked into the public domain. Print and TV media as usual could not help but mess it up. Rumours were peddled. Tempers of the activists went berserk and the authorities realised it was not judicious to arrest Kirtana.

"We may not arrest her. The army has to suggest further course of action," contested the Superintendent of Police.

"It's the call of the state police," an officer from the army took a stand.

An officer mediated, "Instead of arrest, let's take court permission and place them under 'house arrest'. It may pacify the protestors."

* * *

Kirtana and others were placed under 'house arrest'. They were detained in their respective houses with restrictive movements.

Ravindra had just finalised the names of soldiers' to be positioned as security guards at the residences of those placed under 'house arrest'.

He was impatient about beginning the investigation!

He was worried, at the end when the probe was over and the culprits were caught, he had to tackle a tricky situation! He had to declare that Suryam was alive and was honest. It would be celebration time for Suryam. Kirtana would marry Suryam, Ravindra envisioned. He was saddened by the thought of losing Kirtana. He resolved to marry her. It was possible only when Suryam lost the bet. Suryam should exit her life. But HOW? Ravindra ruminated.

He strolled toward Suryam with two cups of tea in his hand. He offered one cup to him.

He noticed Suryam looking sadly at a photo in the newspaper. The photo had Kirtana staring through a window. The caption under the photo read as, 'a *forlorn Kirtana in house arrest!*

Suryam mumbled, "Kirtana is Nature's lover. She loves to be a free bird! Poor fellow, she's kept under house arrest!"

Ravindra heard him.

The neurons in his brain were magically spurred! How about if Suryam was positioned as a 'security guard' at the bungalow of Kirtana? In her proximity, he was sure to breach the agreement. He could not see her suffering. To alleviate her agony, he would surely disclose that he was alive, Ravindra machinated.

* * *

Suryam was wandering in all directions and was returning to the point of picket. It was the point where a security guard should take position. It was the position at the entrance gate of the bungalow of Kirtana!

He was searching for an envelope. He happened to snatch the envelope when he visited his home to console his mother. She was yet to recover from 'the sad loss of her son'. He clutched the envelope while leaving the place.

Unable to find the envelope, Suryam attempted to scratch his head but found a turban coming between his fingers and the skin. He recalled Ravindra covering his head with a wig and a thin cloth and tying it in a knot on top of his head and then wrapping a turban over the knot! A typical Sikh soldier's headgear! Then, Ravindra made Suryam maintain a Sardar beard-another wig-and wear dark 'Ray-ban' glasses! Suryam carefully double-checked the final makeup with great attention to detail. He practised modification in his tone and accent to perfection. He was aware of one of the rules in the bet agreement: **"SURYAM IS RESPONSIBLE FOR ENSURING QUALITY OF THE MAKEUP AND MAINTAIN ANONYMITY"**

Suryam didn't find the envelope. He looked at the wristwatch. It was time he should join Ravindra and go to the police station.

* * *

Sitting on the sofa in her bedroom, Kirtana examined the postal date stamp on the envelope. It was a monthly newsletter sent by the Tata Archery Academy to Suryam. The postal date was as recent as two days ago! She found the newsletter on the ground floor. Her eyes welled up when she saw the name of 'Suryanarayana Thotalli' on the envelope.

How the envelope found its way to her house, she wondered. Suryam was an archer and was trained at the Archery school, Kinnerasani. He was part of the national archery squad. He had been a visiting faculty at the Tata Archery Academy, she recalled.

Her eyes brimmed with tears at the memory of Suryam and his dedication!

The day she visited his place for the first time, she remembered. It was a thatched hut on the banks of Kinnerasani river and it was vividly registered on her mind. Both were studying in Xth class. She hardly noticed him till the day when their maths teacher asked her to rush and inform him that he was selected to represent the Hyderabad Maths Quiz. The only reason the teacher chose her was because it was to be informed urgently and she was the only student in the class who had a two-wheeler. She had a scooty. She played her favourite game, Tennikoit, and returned home. She forgot to inform him about the quiz. She was lazily drooping on the sofa and zapping through the TV channels. She happened to hear on a channel: "Maths Quiz…….." She leapt into the air. She took the Scooty and dashed out. She didn't know where his house was. She remembered the teacher saying, "Suryam lives on the river side. Ask anyone at the river *bund* about him and you will be guided to his house."

Someone guided her. It was a hut. It was close to the upstream. Kinnerasani river was full on the upstream side of the dam. It was dark. She didn't know that there were humans living in absolute darkness without electricity. As she rode further, she heard the sound of gushing river water. Fierce cool breeze twisted her arms. The front tyre skidded. Her Scooty disowned her. She fell and rolled down towards the river side.

It was mud. It was pitch dark. She got up and narrowed her eyes to see better. She saw a disorganised row of huts. An old man saw her falling off the Scooty and helped her. He showed her Suryam's hut!

She managed to walk on the sticky wet black soil. There were no cement walls. It was a thatched hut. She could not find where the entrance door was. She figured out a sort of gap, seemingly a window and peeped through it. Suryam sat on the muddy floor and was studying. An oil lamp was flickering beside him. She surveyed the hut. A pile of firewood, cooking vessels, folded palm leaf mats and two rickety wooden almirahs were evident. Oh my God! There was no electricity. No television!

She heard the voice of a middle-aged female calling his name for help. He ran out and she noticed him climbing the river bund with ease; he scampered up to the female who called him! He received the baggage from her hands. She brought a bundle of grass, a shoal of fish and firewood. As they two returned to the hut, she realised the female was his mother!

She didn't show herself yet. He and his mother ate dinner. His mother gave him the wages of the day which he safe-deposited in the almirah which had no doors to lock! She appeared before him. He was surprised to see her. It was the first time she saw him so close. He was tall and fit. She told him why she had come and she sought his Admission card. Suddenly, there was a commotion. Commotion of dozens of voices screaming, "Run! Run! River is overflowing; take care of the cattle!"

Suryam acted immediately. He read the writing on the wall so fast. He was omnipresent and assisted everyone; he untied the ropes and straps of the cattle and rescued them to safety. He hopped onto a dinghy and went around the river to relieve men and women stuck in the backyards of their huts. He rescued the aged and the deceased. In no time, his friends joined him. Hundreds of men, women, children, cattle, hen, cats, goats, stray dogs and ducks assembled on the river bund.

'Are so many living beings crammed in such a small place?' She was puzzled. The river was swelling fast. She witnessed the fury of Nature for the first time.

He was busy leading the rescue act. She decided to assist him. She managed to obtain his Admission card and rode back to the maths teacher's house.

She reached home late. She was scared her father would grill her. She decided to lie. She didn't realise that way forward she would lie every occasion they met.

Her parents were not awake. She scrambled the stairs quietly and reached her bedroom. Next morning, she planned to bunk the school. She noticed Suryam was going to school. For reasons which she alone could feel but not explain to anyone, she instantly dropped the idea of bunking the school. She never bunked school after that except on days when he too was absent.

He won the quiz. The trophy was showcased in the headmaster's office room.

One night, she got a quirky thought. 'Did he daily and habitually study the school books sitting beside a lamp? Or was the night she saw him for the first time studying in the faint light of a lamp a one-time coincidence? Next moment, she rode to his place. She didn't suspect his sincerity. She just had a dilemma. She had every amenity at her disposal. Yet, she had consistently failed to concentrate.

When she peered secretly through the thatched window, she saw him studying at the lamp with absolute devotion. She also saw a grand drawing on the wall done with charcoal. It was his mom's picture. She learnt from him that he drew it. It was the moment she began to admire him. **It was the day she gave him a pet name-Rishil!**

She made frequent visits to his place. One night, on her request, he took her on the dinghy across the Kinnerasani river. A ride around a thickly vegetated island on the reservoir took them near the dam. The river was lit by self-illuminated stars and moonlight. Hundreds of trees were knitted together to stitch a compact island in the midst of the reservoir. The island, when viewed from the dam against the silhouette of night sky, looked like a birthday cake in dark chocolate decorated on a vast silver coloured sheet of water table. She was bowled over. They strolled on the dam. They rode the dinghy on the reservoir. They halted at the island. They ambled on the island. They rode around on the dinghy and reached home. He said the river was infested with crocodiles. The wilderness of the river did not scare her. She said she felt assured when he was beside her.

Kirtana grieved and cried, as reminiscences of her *Rishil* had intensified. She gazed at his poster!

She peered through the window. Sardar was at the main gate. He was handing over charge to another guard. Not too far back, she found him looking for something in the garden.

* * *

The Circle Inspector of Police (CI) had placed on the table one smudged government file in front of Ravindra and Suryam and explained, "We've one fake notes case. It's a decade ago."

Suryam opened the dusted file. The documents were brittle and were almost torn. It was a complaint about a fake hundred rupees note!

"This file has no relevance for our investigation," Ravindra said, pursing his lips.

"Check with the bank manager. Sometime ago, he mentioned to me a fake currency issue," the CI suggested.

"Is fake currency issue a punishable offence?" Suryam questioned the CI.

"Under IPC Section 489 A, it is punishable with imprisonment and fine," CI clarified, raising his eyebrows.

Ravindra endorsed, "Ya! Sardar! It's a grave offence?"

All the three came out discussing the menace of smuggling! Outside, the CI looked at an Acer transport van! Its tyres were stolen, body was rusted and the vehicle didn't have on it any key automobile part intact! It was abandoned!

He said gesticulating as if he was reminded by something crucial, "Hey! Look at the van! Rumour is it was abandoned by Nagabhushanam. He is a businessman. Gossip is he used it for smuggling currency!"

Suryam said to Ravindra in a lowered tone, "Nagabhushanam is Kirtana's father's name!" and queried the CI in a raised voice, "He abandoned it at the police station?"

"It's a rumour that he abandoned it. There is no proof that the vehicle belonged to him," the CI replied.

"No documents to establish ownership?"

"The number plate was missing. We tried to track its owner based on the chassis number of the engine! The owner and his address were not traceable!"

"What is the basis of a rumour?" Suryam questioned like a prosecutor!

"Anything lacking any basis is called a rumour! Is it not? It's a popular rumour in the town! That's all!" the CI laughed. He noticed his laughter irked Ravindra! Pointing his finger at Suryam and continuing the chuckle, he said, "I'm sorry! The English accent of this Sardar is quite amusing. It's quite funny and lively!"

Ravindra looked at Suryam admiringly for faking the accent so perfectly. From there, he and Suryam drove to meet the bank manager.

* * *

Kirtana lost composure! She felt she forgave her dad when he hired goons to beat Suryam. Suryam too, at her request, was considerate to condone her dad. Both tolerated him. She questioned herself should she now act dumb when she had clear evidence that it was her father who had implicated Suryam in the fake currency case?

Kirtana raged at her dad. Her mother failed to pacify her!

The three were in the bedroom of Kirtana. All doors including the doors of windows were shut.

"Dad, stop bluffing," she argued. "My maths teacher informed me that, a few years ago, he borrowed Rs.30000 from you. The currency notes were found to be fake. Why had you given fake currency to him? I repeated this question a third time and you simply negated it every time! Stop bluffing!"

"I didn't know it was fake. I found the currency in a van," a frustrated Nagabhushanam patiently repeated his reply one more time.

"Dad, I personally met Suryam's father. He confessed that you offered him alcohol and used him to dispatch an envelope to Suryam's army camp address. You sent fake currency in that envelope. You planned to fix Suryam and send him to jail!" Kirtana broke down as he questioned her father!

"Kirtana, you're in blind love with Suryam. I begged you to forget him. I threatened Suryam. He didn't flinch. Nothing worked. I had no doubt he had an eye on our properties. I thought, as a last resort, I should bribe him with something valuable. I dispatched a gift deed of expensive land! I wrote to him to accept the gift and forget you forever!"

"Dad, you're lying!! The army claimed that it had found fake currency in that envelope!" Kirtana cried.

"................" Nagabhushanam shook his head in disapproval!

"Dad, you abandoned a van! You used the van for smuggling currency!?"

"I was made to abandon it. I didn't smuggle any currency!"

"Dad, you're a liar, liar, liar!" Kirtana shouted, sobbing loudly.

Staring at nothingness, Nagabhushanam stood up. He could not stomach his daughter's accusation. He walked dejectedly out of her bedroom, expedited the pace of his walking as he was climbing down the stairs, decisively dashed into his room, vigorously slammed the doors behind him. He did not switch on the lights. He hammered the doors of the windows to shut.

A few minutes later, Suryam was banging on the door of the room of Nagabhushanam. Kirtana and her mother rushed down. They saw Sardar breaking open the doors and there they saw Nagabhushanam attempting suicide by hanging to the ceiling fan!

Suryam rescued him! He saw a disconsolate Kirtana. *'It's impossible for me to see her suffering,'* he considered.

He stopped in the doorway, turned around and without looking at Kirtana, he said unpretentiously, "Ma'am! In my opinion, your dad may be given patient listening."

Kirtana replied with a tremble in her voice, "Thank you!"

Kirtana's mother folded her palms together and showed her gratitude. Suryam smiled hesitantly, moved swiftly and walked back to the picket point.

"I'm not lying Kirtana! I've nothing to do with fake currency!" Nagabhushanam slumped into a chair, hid his face in both his palms and sobbed like a child.

* * *

Overwhelmed with disbelief, Suryam became numb. *"What's happening?'* he muttered. At the entrance gate of the bungalow, in the garden lit by the dim light of a gate lamp, feeling emotionally constricted, he attempted to pass his hands through his hair, rub the scalp and relieve himself from a severe feeling of stress. The turban and the wig came in his way. He extended his arms straight above his head and tried to find physical relief. He stretched his arms away from his torso as tight as he could and relaxed.

'Why Nagabhushanam attempted suicide?'

He stared at Nagabhushanam's room. He saw Kirtana and her mother consoling him!

'I even prepared, at the behest of Ravindra, a charge sheet accusing him! Is Nagabhushanam innocent?'

He bent his body backwards, arched his body like a bow and touched the ground with his open palms.

'Oh my god! Had I not seen, he might have committed suicide!'

He took a deep breath, returned to his normal stance, stood erect, raised his gaze toward the dark sky, straightened his left arm in front of him, aimed an imaginary arrow and released it into the emptiness when he considered he attained focus!

'Am I wrong? Is he innocent?' he reviewed.

He recalled the meeting with the bank manager in the afternoon. The manager informed him that a few years ago, cash was deposited by a customer. The cashier found it as fake currency. The customer informed the cashier that he received it from Nagabhushanam. Nagabhushanam visited the bank, pleaded ignorance and compensated the Bank.

When Suryam queried the cashier who that customer was, he learnt it was his maths teacher!

He knew why the maths teacher took money from Nagabhushanam. Suryam had no money to join the college. He decided to discontinue studies and join as a labourer at a paddy farm. His maths teacher had come forward to support. He paid tuition and examination fees. He borrowed to pay fees. Later, when Suryam received his salary, he offered to pay back the debt. The maths teacher said that there was no urgency. He asked Suryam to use his savings to construct a pucca house for his mother. Every time he cited an excuse to not accept the refund from Suryam.

Suryam, disguised as a Sikh sepoy, met his teacher today. He lied to the teacher that Suryam's mother gave him cash to settle the debt. The teacher did not accept the refund. He cried in repentance. He regretted, "Sardar! I never supported Suryam. It was always Kirtana. When Suryam refused to accept her support, she requested me to act as the donor. I borrowed and paid the tuition fees. On due dates, she gave me money to settle the instalments." The teacher felt sad that Suryam would never know that Kirtana supported his education.

Suryam was moved to learn that Kirtana supported his education. He asked his teacher, "Sir, the bank manager informed me a fake currency issue happened at the bank?"

The teacher looked surprised. "Damn bank manager! Has he let you know it? When he kept you posted about it, has he not bothered to let you also know who compensated it?"

Suryam responded that he said it was a businessman by the name Nagabhushanam.

'Yes! People say Nagabhushanam smuggles currency," said a disturbed teacher.

Suryam and Ravindra analysed that every finger was pointing to Nagabhushanam. They decided to meet

Suryam's father. Their suspicion was that, enticed by alcohol, Suryam's father had divulged the camp address of Suryam to an unscrupulous fellow who in turn dispatched fake currency to Suryam's address. The official camp addresses of military staff were coded and were privy to the department staff and members of the family. When Ravindra and Suryam met Suryam's father, they found him fully drunk. They thought they would interrogate him the next day.

Suryam paused the physical stretches at the entrance gate and pondered over his dilemma. *'Should I stop the investigation after the interrogation of my dad? Should I not look at the evidence more closely? There is more to something than meets the eye, I am sure!'* He felt relieved only when he resolved that he should deep dive the case.

CHAPTER 4

Drama at the Downstream Riverbed

Suryam was riding the bike with full steam racing through dry bushes on either side of the dusty narrow rural roads! The sun was scorching hot. Nagabhushanam was the pillion rider! In the dry riverbed downstream of Kinnerasani dam, he finished the ride at a neglected and deserted hamlet!

A drained Nagabhushanam got off the two-wheeler. Clueless, he questioned, "Sardar, why have you rescued me from the police?"

"I believe you're not the culprit," Suryam replied, wiping sweat off his brow. He surveyed around, noticed no trace of humans in the vicinity, felt safe and sat on a rock.

A few feet away there was an uninhabited house under the shade of a massive *Neem* tree. The house had a tiled-roof and wore a vintage look.

Suryam adjusted the turban, scratched his fake beard to relieve the itchy sensation, puckered his lips in circular motions, moistening them to alleviate the sense of thirst.

Far away, on one side Kinnerasani dam was seen and on the other side of the horizon, green hills dotted the landscape.

Suspecting foul play, Nagabhushanam asked, "Sardar! Why do you believe I'm not the culprit? Why this soft corner for me?"

Suryam thought he should first win the trust of Nagabhushanam. He nodded, gesturing that he owed to offer an answer and narrated, "Sir! Apart from Suryam, two more soldiers were accused. Envelopes were delivered to them also. Intelligence Services found fake currency in those envelopes also. The two soldiers were immediately arrested. An investigation was ordered to enquire who sent the envelopes!" He paused as he noticed Nagabhushanam had a question.

Nagabhushanam intervened, "I'm sure, a fraudster approached their families and obtained their camp addresses!"

"Interestingly, no one approached. I met the families of the arrested two. They confirmed that none approached them seeking the camp address of the two. It means an insider from the military, in connivance with the mafia, may have plotted a nasty plan. I understood we should dig into the case. My boss, Ravindra disagreed. He believed we have clinching evidence to arrest you. He ordered me to file a chargesheet with the CI. I didn't file. I decided to pursue the case on my own!"

Nagabhushanam looked at ease. His face lit up. His eyes illuminated. "Thanks, Sardar, for deciding to probe the case more logically," he praised.

However, Nagabhushanam told himself incredulously, *"Ravindra wanted me to be arrested!?! No way!"*

"Sir! I need you to answer my questions before I absolve you!" Suryam stared at Nagabhushanam.

Nagabhushanam bobbed his head showing his intent to answer sincerely. He indicated he was feeling acutely thirsty! Hot wind was blowing across the empty river bed.

There was an earthen pot with drinking water inside it in the house nearby. There were tumblers also. Suryam knew it. He was visiting that spot, of late, quite often. He felt it was naive on his part to bring potable water in a steel tumbler from that abandoned house and offer it to Nagabhushanam! He restrained himself though he too was feeling unbearable thirst.

"What questions?" Nagabhushanam asked, rubbing the sweat over his face with a kerchief.

"Sir, why have you obtained Suryam's camp address from his father?" Suryam questioned.

"Oh! It's a crazy thing I did, Sardar! Kirtana fell in love with Suryam. He was from a low caste and labour class," Nagabhushanam's face took on a stern and unyielding look at the mere mention of Suryam's name and he continued, "I tried to disrupt their relationship. It didn't work. Kirtana was in mad love with him. Suryam trapped Kirtana. He had an eye on my property. I thought I should offer a hefty bribe to keep him away from my family. I dispatched a gift deed to Suryam. It was a gift of valuable land. I wrote to him to accept the gift and leave my daughter forever. I obtained Suryam's camp address from his father and dispatched the envelope!"

Suryam felt dumbfounded. He sighed deeply and asked with a stoic face, "You abandoned a van? You used it for smuggling currency?"

Nagabhushanam looked puzzled. He shook his head and clarified assertively, "I bought it in a *sale* from a used-vehicle dealer in Hyderabad. I paid Rs. 3 lac and drove it home. Two days later, the dealer said he could not complete the registration formalities and advised me not to contact him anymore. I sought the documents of the previous owner. He stopped responding to my calls.

"Meanwhile, I found currency notes tied together valuing Rs.2 lakhs stuck in a corner inside the van. I was glad it was a lucky van! I pestered the dealer for completion of registration formalities.

"One day a person came. He gave me Rs. 3 lakhs and said, "This is the money you paid for the van." He didn't seek the return of the van. Instead, he threw at me a piece of paper with words written on it, *'abandon the van.'*

"Incidentally, that afternoon, the maths teacher borrowed Rs. 30000 from me. I unintentionally gave him currency notes that I found in the van! The teacher later complained that the cash he received from me was fake notes. I exchanged good money. I burnt the entire Rs. 2 lakhs of fake currency in my backyard! I abandoned the van. I never smuggled currency!"

Suryam felt he had no more questions. He saw a sequentially logical and truthful confession flowing from Nagabhushanam like a river inundated by a bout of pure rain water falling in cadence from the heavens! He said, "Sir, I'm convinced!"

"Thanks! Sardar, I have one suggestion. Take your boss into confidence. Ravindra is a Major and senior to you. Do the investigation under his guidance!"

"It's difficult to convince my boss at this point!" Suryam declared.

Suddenly, Suryam rose, scampered up to the bike and kick-started it. He observed at a distance a white SUV that seemed to belong to Kirtana approaching. It was coming in their direction slowly negotiating the sand and the pebbles. He hurried Nagabhushanam to occupy the pillion. He drove the bike away from the house, that neem tree, that rock and that deserted hamlet! That house was the secret spot Kirtana and Suryam met often in yesteryears.

Suryam halted the bike where he felt it was safe.

Moments later, he saw Kirtana stepping out of the SUV. She craned her neck in all directions and spotted them.

She screamed, "Dad! Come over here. The car will not reach there!"

Pointing at something in the sky, she shouted, "Look up! Something is flying!"

Suryam noticed a drone at a distance flying randomly. He recognised it was an army drone! He grasped the danger he was running into, *'Ravindra seems approaching. He's hell bent to arrest Nagabhushanam.'*

Suryam thrusted his two-wheeler to the ground. He decided he should relinquish it there. He held Nagabhushanam's hand and sped toward Kirtana.

When they reached the van, Suryam hastened, "Let's leave this place immediately!"

"Are we going home?" Kirtana questioned grimly as she had no clue why Sardar picked her father on his bike and left the bungalow in a hurry without informing her or her mother!

Nagabhushanam already sat beside the driver seat and was quenching thirst by slugging down *Bisleri* water. He glanced at Suryam hinting that Suryam should answer. Suryam decisively replied, "Ma'am, we shall go to Hyderabad."

Kirtana incredulously looked at both. "I should know why you came to this spot?" she insisted.

"Ma'am, the police were set to arrest your dad with half-baked evidence. I thought I should rescue him. Your dad is crucial for pursuing my probe! Please start the vehicle now," Suryam pleaded.

Kirtana looked at her father. Nagabhushanam gulped a bottle of water and belched. He pouted his lips back and forth and said, "I don't know what to say. Sardar says his boss sent the police to arrest me. Why will Ravindra get me arrested when…..." Kirtana reacted quickly and didn't allow her dad to finish. She overrode her dad's voice and said loudly, "Let's leave this place."

She imagined, *"Dad, I know why Ravindra is in a hurry to get you arrested! He wants to spot the criminal before I do!"*

She thumped on the gear stick and pressed on the accelerator.

Nagabhushanam felt sandwiched. He reasoned Ravindra should be trusted and taken into confidence. He was certain that Kirtana would hate it! He also rationalised that Sardar's exploration seemed to be heading in the right direction. *'Sardar rightly explained to me why we should go to Hyderabad! So far so good! But how nice it is more if Sardar takes guidance from his boss and Kirtana starts befriending Ravindra!'* he fancied.

Kirtana checked through the rear-view mirror. Sardar was not visible. Suryam chose to sit in the left corner of the middle seat to hide himself from the sight of Kirtana. Kirtana felt hesitant to look back. She discreetly gave him a sidelong glance and registered a slim and muscular object in an army uniform with a Punjabi headgear! *'Sardars will normally have a hefty physique!'* she doubted.

"Dad, I saw Sardar and you fleeing on a bike. I found it hard to chase you! I went in the wrong direction for quite some time. Why did you choose the downstream? You guided him to the riverbed? or Sardar brought you here?" Kirtana questioned as she steered the vehicle onto the road.

Nagabhushanam, having had no clue why Sardar brought him to the riverbed, looked back suggesting to Suryam it was his responsibility to respond to that question! Suryam bobbed his head in agreement and replied, "Ma'am, I drove your dad here. Jungle-like places are safe to hide from the police. Civil police normally avoid forests!"

"Why have you saved my dad from the police?" Kirtana questioned as she escalated the speed of the vehicle.

Although Suryam put in great effort to modify his tone and accent, it still required a lot of skill, focus and concentration to keep it up. As he reflected on the sequence of events that he wanted to share with Kirtana, he was making sure to speak in a pleasant and engaging manner.

Meanwhile, Nagabhushanam gestured to Suryam that he would better clarify it to his daughter. Devoid of clutter in his head, a confident Nagabhushanam refreshed, readjusted himself in the seat and narrated. He detailed to her point by point why Sardar believed he was not guilty!

As Nagabhushanam narrated, Suryam leaned forward attentively, nodding in agreement and showing his sincere interest. When Nagabhushanam finished, Suryam made a thoughtful conclusion, "Let me clear the air. I've nothing against my supervisor! At this moment, his judgement is absolutely wrong! I will prove my point!"

The SUV was going at a galloping speed.

"How long shall we hide from the police?' Kirtana doubted.

"Maybe a day or two!" Suryam simplified.

"Where are we headed now?" Kirtana screeched impatiently.

"To Hyderabad," Suryam explained.

"Why to Hyderabad?" Her voice was stern.

Nagabhushanam intervened again, "Sardar already clarified to me why Hyderabad. He has a point. We shall go to Hyderabad and meet……"

Kirtana blared the horn to alert a car ahead of them.

Nagabhushanam felt due to the grating noise of the horn, he was not heard! He tried to repeat. She said, "Dad, I heard you. I'm okay as long as the purpose is to nab the culprit!' and she pressed on the accelerator. *I'm doubly keen to catch the gangster before Ravindra does! It is crucial to my life,' she worried.*

"I guess we're not being tracked." Nagabhushanam asked.

"Power off your phones. Ravindra is authorised to track phones. Do not switch on unless we've a dire need!" Suryam suggested.

"Are you a Punjabi? Or an Assamese? You wore a turban and your accent is Punjabi. You have a button nose like a northeast guy!" Kirtana smiled as she enquired.

"I'm your Rishil, Kirtana!" Suryam felt like screaming loudly. He refrained when rules of the bet agreement between him and Ravindra spawned on his mind for the millionth time.

He tapped his nose and felt the tiny smooth clip made of soft skin like material. *"That button nose is not required for a Punjabi image; You remove it,*" Ravindra suggested and Suryam had forgotten while applying makeup!

"My father is a Punjabi and my mother is an Assamese!' Suryam tried to balance!

He opened his purse and took out a colour photo and showed it to Kirtana's dad and said, "Me and my dad!" Suryam manipulated a photo of himself in Punjabi makeup and mixed it with a fifty-five-year-old genetically genuine Punjabi male and photoshopped a *son-and-dad* photo!

Nagabhushanam peered at it and said appreciatively, "You resemble your dad!" and passed the photo to Kirtana. Kirtana had a quick glance at it. She tried to observe his nose in the photo but the image was a little blurry.

After a while, Nagabhushanam said, "I switched off phones." He secured them in the glove box.

What Kirtana and Suryam didn't notice was that Nagabhushanam managed to send a WhatsApp message to Ravindra's father.

Since Ravindra, for defence security reasons, should not routinely be sent WhatsApp messages, Nagabhushanam had always texted to Ravindra's father to communicate with their family. He sent a message, *"Sir! All is well. Me and Kirtana on the way to Hyderabad. Please inform Ravindra. Regards."*

* * *

Ravindra pressed the 'back' button of the controller. The drone stopped hovering and reached the spot where Ravindra halted his SUV. He rolled down the window, collected the drone and drove ahead. The drone sent fragmented images as it flew back and forth.

'Uncle's phone registered this location! Where is he?' an irate Ravindra looked around. Blazing hot air was discharging through his ears. He observed the trace of tyres on a patch of sand. He stepped out. He followed the tracks by foot. He covered a distance and detected a bike lying flat on its side. It was the bike of Suryam! He noticed footsteps on the sand. He marched furlongs downstream toward the parched riverbed. He paused at a *Neem* tree. He felt desperate to take a break under its cool shade. He observed marks of army shoes. *'Suryam surely came here!'* Ravindra assessed.

He spotted a coir rope hanging from the *Neem* tree branch. He pulled it and a cloth hammock had at once dropped in front of him. A cotton saree was fastened to the tree and used as a swing. The saree had a peacock border. A vivid memory of a photo in an album came rushing back as he saw a peacock bordered saree. He recalled seeing it on Kirtana! He was stunned. *'Is it Kirtana's saree?'* He brushed the saree swing aside.

He located a deserted house and walked toward it. Interestingly, contrary to his expectation, the house inside was tidy and well maintained as if someone was residing there. There were two rooms side by side and a kitchen room in the backyard.

He stepped into a room. He shuddered to see Kirtana! He stepped back in shock! He soon realised it was a life-size drawing of Kirtana on the white washed wall. It was drawn with charcoal. It looked real! She was clad in saree, stood on a dinghy smiling like a jasmine, looking at someone and extended her arm offering a lotus flower! The tranquillity of the river reflected in the background! Ravindra fell head over heels at the sight of her fabulous picture! He walked close to her picture and felt her beauty with his hands! *'What a gorgeous lady? She was offering a lotus flower to whom?' he cooed.* The drawing on the wall extended into the other room. Ravindra followed it. He entered the second room. He saw on the wall the picture of a young man sitting on one knee on the other end of the dinghy and extended his arm accepting to receive the lotus flower! He was like Suryam! Ravindra felt paranoid!

He noticed the room had two cane chairs! Country wood handpicked from *Neem* tree branches were nailed into the wall that looked like a shelf! A plastic miniature of a cute boy in a cap and a girl in short gown smooching each other decorated the shelf. Ravindra recalled a similar toy decorating the shelf in the bedroom of Kirtana! His heart buckled with jealousy.

He saw a mirror and makeup material! He felt sure that Suryam, of late, was visiting the place often! *'He is picking on the variations of the art of makeup too soon, I believe!'* he grumbled.

He entered the kitchen room. He saw an earthen pot and steel tumblers. He drew aside the plate on the pot and found water! He quenched thirst. He noticed firewood, earthen stove, a pan, a coffee kettle, tin of oil, salt, red chilli powder etc.

He felt he heard the voice of Kirtana laughing charmingly. He turned around. He saw Suryam hugging Kirtana from behind. Suryam wrapped his arms around her warmly. She caressed his arms to show she liked his endearing hug. Ravindra shook his head off disbelievingly. He cursed his imagination!

He suspected, *'Is this Suryam and Kirtana's meeting spot?'* He turned green with envy!

He poured red chilli powder and water on the picture of Suryam. He smeared it beyond recognition. He observed a name written on the side of the dinghy where Suryam knelt! It was, *'Kirtana'*. He didn't erase her name.

He went back to the first room to see whose name was written on the side of the dinghy where she stood! He anticipated it to be *'Suryam'*. He found it as: *'Rishil'*

'Who is Rishil?' Does Kirtana have another boyfriend? Is Suryam not her boyfriend? He is, of course! I saw his poster in her bedroom. Is Rishil ex of Kirtana? Can Suryam draw

pictures? I don't know this side of his personality!' Ravindra felt muddled.

He stood in front of the picture of Kirtana. He adored her! *'She is a supermodel!'* His desire to marry her mounted.

His mind spurred the urgent task to arrest Nagabhushanam. Nagabhushanam should be arrested and be grilled to crack the scam; he was deeply convinced.

After Nagabhushanam's arrest, he schemed, he would be the default guardian to Kirtana and her properties. Her parents and his parents were anyway with him to tie the alliance. She might put up a token resistance and go through the motions. It was a matter of time she too fell in line, he sensed.

He doubted what would happen to Suryam? Would Kirtana not choose him as the default guardian of hers?

Suryam dug his own grave, Ravindra contemplated! Suryam saved Nagabhushanam, the accused. For such connivance, he would go to jail or had to abscond and live incognito forever!

Ravindra was annoyed that Suryam not only protected Nagabhushanam but also had gone too far as to dare to provide guidance to him on how to conduct the probe. He recalled Suryam's advice: *"Sir, please check with our Intelligence Services. Two envelopes should have been delivered in my name. One will have fake currency and the other a gift deed. Nagabhushanam dispatched a gift deed to me. Please inform me when you receive the confirmation. Till then, Nagabhushanam shall be in my custody!"*

Ravindra blew a gasket. He roared, "Suryam, hell with your guidance! You leave the investigation to me. You surrender Nagabhushanam to me. Where are you?"

His roar echoed in the empty house!

He walked out of the house. His foremost task was to trace Nagabhushanam. He considered sharing his photographs with the television media and let the media announce that Nagabhushanam was eluding the police. The news should go live on all channels, he resolved.

He saw an incoming call. It was from his father!

CHAPTER 5

Journey to Hyderabad not Without Hitches

The SUV was zooming on the highway toward Hyderabad. Suryam sat like a prince. Buoyant, cheerful, relaxed and in control of the situation! He sat in the middle row so close behind Kirtana and was observing her with a caring gaze. She was driving with focus.

He leaned back, adjusted his head on the headrest and closed his eyes.

That was a story of difficult choices. Seven years ago, he wrote the NEET exam at the request of Kirtana, achieved top rank and admission to Vellore Medical College. However, to join the college, he required a few lakhs which was promised by the maths teacher. In reality, it was only yesterday that he learned the truth that it was Kirtana, not his teacher, who had been supporting him financially all these years. Meanwhile, his father informed him that his uncle Veeraiah was willing to help, which initially brought him joy. He soon discovered that the offer came with a condition; in exchange, he would have to agree to marry Veeraiah's blind daughter, Madhavi. Suryam refused the proposal, not because of Madhavi's blindness, but because he was committed to Kirtana and was in a relationship with her.

Madhavi was a beloved member of the household. Suryam was deeply saddened when he inadvertently became involved in an embarrassing situation due to a false promise made by his father to his uncle while under the influence of alcohol. When he said NO to Madhavi, Veeraiah withdrew support. Suryam felt it agonising. He was hesitant to seek help from his teacher. Instead, he left home in a fit of anger and frustration and happened to cross the archery school where the Indian army was conducting selections for new recruits. In a moment of impulse, he decided to register his name and pursue a career in the military. When he later texted Kirtana an SMS that he had decided to join the army as sepoy and pleaded with her to forgive him and forget him, she replied back: *'RISHIL, YOU MAY BECOME A DOCTOR OR DRIVER OF A TRACTOR OR A SOLDIER. IT MATTERS LITTLE TO ME ABOUT WHAT YOU ARE! WE LIVE FOR EACH OTHER AND ONE DAY WE SHALL GET MARRIED!"*

Suryam opened eyes. He glanced at Kirtana with a look of admiration. He took pleasure in the fact that she completed her MBBS and became a qualified doctor. Despite her immense success, she never once looked down on him or tried to distance herself from their relationship. Her sincere nature left him in awe, and he couldn't help but admire her even more.

Kirtana made sense of Sardar watching her. She moved her gaze at him for a moment. She saw Sardar taking his eyes off her and looking straight ahead! *'Sardar has sported dark ray-ban glasses inside a car?'* she wondered. She tidied up her churidar, sat erect and turned her attention to the highway.

She recalled one day Sardar searching for something in the garden. It was the day she found an envelope containing a newsletter sent by Tata Archery Academy to Suryam. She kept that newsletter on her study table. She found it missing a day after!

Last night, she noticed Sardar doing body stretching at the entrance gate; she noticed him releasing an imaginary arrow! *'His stance is Rishil like'* she felt.

Sardar drove her dad to the location close to THEIR meeting spot a while ago, she wondered. Her sixth sense began to transmit. It ushered in an intuition. At once, the casket with mortal remains of Suryam lying in the mortuary of the government hospital manifested in her consciousness. It sent tears in her eyes. She found it difficult to drive.

"Shall we have coffee?" she asked.

"Is it safe to halt?" Suryam doubted.

"A quick sip of coffee is okay!" Nagabhushanam mediated.

Kirtana stopped at a highway cafeteria abutting a petrol station. They had coffee. Suryam had a good memory of her coffee preferences and routinely ordered it for her. She was surprised at it.

The petrol tank was filled. Kirtana affected payments through Phone Pay.

The three were yet to get inside the car. Evening wind was blowing gently across the parking space.

"Do you know Suryam very well?" Kirtana enquired Sardar adjusting the strands of her hair that had fallen onto her face.

"Yes, of course! We belonged to the same unit!" Suryam asserted.

Suryam sensed Kirtana was watching him! He thought it was the right time. He was waiting for such a moment. He took out a manipulated colour photograph from his purse and showed it to her.

Kirtana glanced at it. The photo had Suryam and Sardar standing in an open lawn area with their arms around each other. Both were in army uniform. Sardar had a headgear, moustache and dark glasses; Suryam wore a cap and a bright smile.

The photoshopped photo had images of Suryam disguised as Sardar and real Suryam together in the same photo. "We took this photo when we were at Dehradun camp!" Suryam told her.

She liked it. She was about to ask, "May I keep this photo with me?" Her dad seized it. He stared at it irritably. He didn't like the sight of Suryam in the photo. He frowned, abruptly returned it to Suryam and said, "Sardar, let's go!" Kirtana refrained from seeking the photo!

Suryam was disappointed. He had twin purposes when he showed the photo to her. It would erase any iota of intuition that might be creeping into the mind of Kirtana to suspect the gait of Sardar!

Secondly, he yearned that she sought the photo and preserved it as a souvenir in his memory. He worried if she was beginning to forget about him.

They were about to resume the journey. Kirtana threw the keys at Suryam and said, "Sardar, will you please drive! I'm tired!" She sat in the middle row. Suryam took to driving!

* * *

"Major! I couldn't arrest Nagabhushanam. He was not at home. His wife had no clue where he was; we are searching for him," Circle Inspector advised Ravindra.

'I know you are not able to arrest him,' Ravindra told himself. He was sure Nagabhushanam was the culprit. However, he himself didn't want to arrest him and antagonise Kirtana and her mother. Hence, he filed a chargesheet at the police station and roped in the CI to deal with the arrest of Nagabhushanam.

"Oh inspector! Has he escaped?" Ravindra sounded surprised.

The CI asked with a cold voice, "Sir, where are you?"

Ravindra doubted whether he should disclose where he was heading! He replied, "Not audible! Network issue! I will call you back!"

The CI felt ignored. He felt the police were undervalued by the army right from day one of the investigation. He knew Ravindra was on the highway. *'Where is he driving without searching for Nagabhushanam?'* he doubted. He was circumspect and was approaching the matter with utmost caution. He adopted token engagement with the case. It was a case, he felt, which had sensitivities like fake currency, a deceased soldier who was alleged to have links with mafia, a local police unit which had no information of the past history of Nagabhushanam-the accused and Kirtana who seemed to be a social activist! What began as a local law and order case was heading its way to Hyderabad, he thought.

Ravindra was driving very fast toward Hyderabad. His dad informed about Nagabhushanam's WhatsApp message. Ravindra was amazed why Kirtana and her dad headed to Hyderabad. He contacted them but to no avail. He doubted whether Suryam also accompanied them. Had Suryam blatantly dumped the bet? Had he revealed to Kirtana that he was alive?

He sent an email to his close friend, a Regional News Editor on a media channel. "Hi! buddy, I have attached a photo. He is Nagabhushanam from Paloncha town and is wanted in a scam. Please telecast his photo and announce that he is eluding the police! I'm in charge of the investigation!"

The tracker registered Kirtana's location. It was a cafeteria on the highway. He drove in that direction.

* * *

Retail shop after shop engaged in tourism pastime shopping, abutting one another with no cement walls to define their boundaries were trading folklore items on either side of the narrow lane opposite Mahabaleswara temple, Gokarna, Karnataka state.

Traders were busy selling handicrafts, musical instruments like drums and sitars to guitars, jewellery made of conchs and sea shells, spices of India, T shirts, palm hats, trendy skirts, night gowns, vintage books, *Tantrik* photos, benzoin resin extracted from a tree *(sambrani)*. The place was buzzing with tourists.

Kirtana walked into a clothes shop; she was searching for a sea blue colour skirt. A romantic song was being played from the Ek Duje Ke Liye movie and the loudspeaker placed at the entrance of the shop amplified SPB's soulful voice. Skirts and gowns were hung to the hangers in a zigzag pattern and she marched through the hangers in the shop which had as many hairpin bends as a narrow ghat road. She went up to the last hanger searching for the blue colour skirt and it was dark at that far end. She went so far inside the shop; the song was less audible.

Someone held her from behind, lifted her up and hugged her. She screamed in panic and turned her head to see. Suryam was smiling! She was taken aback. She rejoiced! "Rishil! You?! What a surprise?" Holding his hand, she turned around like in a ballroom dance and looked into his eyes. His curly dark hair was a treat to her eyes! She brushed his hair fondly with her fingers. His smile arrested her. She stroked on his lower lip with her right-hand index finger as if a guitar player would stroke the strings while finetuning it. He was chewing bubble gum! His jaw muscles were spotted by her! She gently raised on her toes and kissed his cheeks!

He embraced her! They wrapped themselves in each other's arms. The noise of someone approaching was heard! He smoothly set her back down. She asked, "Rishil! How come you are here!?"

His happiness too had no bounds. "You should have guessed when a song from Ek Duje Ke Liye had been played. I requested the shop owner to play it," he said with a playful smile on his face and continued, "I was sanctioned leave. I know you're here. I thought I'd surprise you!"

"Catch me," she cheered, felt ecstatic and scooted out. He scampered behind her. She sprinted to the seashore facing the Mahabaleshwar temple. It was evening at 6 p.m. The twilight sun was descending at the sandy shore! Lengthy shadows reflected on the wet sand. "Catch my shadow, if you can," Kirtana bid and ran! She romped gleefully meandering through the crowds at the beach. Dashing behind her, he was mesmerised by her hourglass like figure and marble-soft skin decked in a cotton saree. They had run along the shore. Their minds were saturated with mirth and joy!

She held the folds of the saree in her right hand, eased her pace of running movement and sprinted back to the shopping area. She stood at a tattoo designer shop and called Suryam to join. From there they went together hand in hand walking, sprinting, laughing, tittering, jogging, ambling and strolling from one beach to the other. Their hearts were racing. Time was racing to catch up with them.

At Om beach they thought they would have dinner. It was 9 p.m. An unimaginable count of crowds swelled the beach; boys and girls were boozing; smokers were puffing out cigar smoke in billows. DJ music was reverberating! Kirtana and Suryam were so excited and thrilled that they were looking for an isolated and tranquil location to relax and converse. Their eyes giggled and communicated with each other. They ran away from there.

They stopped at a tea stall. It was 10 p.m. They enjoyed hot omelettes and tea. They continued strolling.

Night sky lit by the moon and the stars was like a pool of liquid mercury. Kirtana and Suryam decided to ascend a hillock. Cool breeze stood company to them. They reached the Small Hell beach. It was a rocky surface with narrow gorges to be negotiated carefully. Waves were surging into the narrow caves; water was gushing up the gorge and splashing out into the open space as if gas in the soda bottle escaped making hissing noise!

When Kirtana was not able to climb the slopes, Suryam carried her.

Kirtana saw a bunch of fruits looking like tiny apples rolled and piled in a corner. The fruits were shining under the moonlight. Suryam saw her picking a fruit. He seized her hand, grasped the fruit and threw it afar. "It's a strychnine fruit. Very poisonous. One fruit is enough to take away your life!" Suryam cautioned.

"Oh my god! I can't believe it. How do you know it?" Kirtana asked with a surprise.

"We are trained to know about the basics of forest and wildlife!" Suryam told her.

Wind was thrusting sea water to the shore as if trying to mix the sea water with the sand at the beach and gushy noise of waves was echoing in the open space. Kirtana and Suryam stood together on top of a hillock with the sea on all sides shining gloriously.

They ambled around. After an hour when they returned to the spot where Kirtana picked a strychnine fruit, she saw there were no fruits now. "Oye! No fruits!" she screamed. Suryam showed a cluster of birds with large yellow beaks perched on the branches of the strychnine fruit tree and said, "It's their food! It's a bird called Toucan."

Whispers emanating from the lips of the young couple urged the wind to listen silently to their words! Kirtana surrendered into the hug of Suryam. She said, "It's midnight. It's a forest. Are we safe?" Suryam closed her lips with his, kissed her tight and replied, "We are safe as long as we are together!

Kirtana opened her eyes. She visited Gokarna with her college classmates on an excursion. Suryam joined her and they had a lifetime experience at Gokarna! Tears rolled down her cheeks uncontrollably. She cried silently, *"Rishil! You promised we will live together!"*

She checked her tears. She saw Sardar driving the SUV attentively and her dad snoozing.

* * *

Ravindra noticed an incoming call from the CI.

A while ago, the CI had seen news being telecast on a TV channel that Nagabhushanam went absconding and was elusive to the police. He had come to know that it was Ravindra who raised the issue to the media.

"Any more news about Nagabhushanam?" the CI enquired. Ravindra said no.

But he had crucial news to report. He was not ready to share an important piece of information with the CI that he received from his colleague from the Intelligence Services. He was informed that there were two envelopes delivered to the camp address of Suryam. One envelope had fake currency and another envelope had a gift deed.

After receiving the information, Ravindra felt like a fish out of water. He realised Nagabhushanam did not seem to be the culprit. Suryam said it right. There was someone else. He grew anxious. He should in fact advise the CI to stop tracking Nagabhushanam. He didn't! He had a bigger issue at hand now! Had Suryam gathered more evidence to crack the case? He was upset. He knew he could not tolerate if Suryam singlehandedly unravelled the case. His credibility was at stake. He was certain that he should lead the investigation, at any cost. He should at least appear to have led it. Would it sound like a scenario of 'stolen credit' for Suryam's performance, he introspected. No way! He believed that he had been guiding Suryam right from the start. However, it was Suryam who made the choice to go against his instructions. As per the code of conduct, Suryam should acknowledge his mistake and let him lead and guide him instead, he reasoned.

He slammed down the accelerator pedal and was zooming at mad speed. He didn't know where to go. Fervently hoping that he would get access to their location he was driving the vehicle in the direction of Hyderabad.

* * *

The SUV was crawling at a snail's pace in the twin cities traffic. Kirtana heard Sardar humming a tune and tapping on the steering wheel with his fingers rhythmically. She grasped what tune it was! Suryam used to hum it and drum it on the steering wheel.

She asked, "Sardar! What song is it?"

Suryam suddenly realised he was caught in a situation without being prepared for it! He didn't know any Punjabi songs or any names of popular Punjabi singers to babble out some names! He was spontaneously not able to remember any other singer's name or any other song! It appeared as if he lost memory! He felt he remembered the name of only one singer and only one tune and it was the one that he was humming and drumming at the moment. He could ill afford to disclose that song to Kirtana! He deliberately turned to Nagabhushanam and asked, "How far is the dealer showroom?"

Nagabhushanam raised his chin up, made a few calculations and replied, "Just one more kilometre!"

Suryam used that time to make an alteration in the rhythm of the tune! He looked around and saw a Shirdi Sai temple on the roadside. He shifted to humming a Sai Bhajan and replied to Kirtana, "Ma'am! It's Shirdi Sai Bhajan!"

Kirtana could hardly believe it. She heard him humming the song from the movie Ek Duje Ke Liye! It was Suryam's favourite number. *'Who is Sardar?'* she wondered. Her brain ushered in to intuit.

Kirtana gave Suryam a warm hug. They were at the riverbed under the Neem tree! He was humming a song he most liked! She asked him, "What you liked most about that movie! It's a tragedy!" "I too don't know! Every time I listen to those songs, I feel I'm in more love with you!" he replied. "Don't ever leave me, Rishil!" She looked at him hard.

Kirtana glanced at Sardar as she heard the same humming once more. Suryam was unknowingly and habitually back to humming the *Ek Duje Ke Liye* song and drumming it on the steering wheel! A few tunes were like earworms and catchy and would be played unconsciously.

In the back of Kirtana's subconscious mind, a fleeting moment seemed to capture a known image as she looked at Sardar! Her heart sank! An extrasensory perception was about to hint something indescribable.

At once, her emotion drove her memory circuits to the Suryam's casket lying in the government mortuary! Sixth sense was auto-shut down! The image of Suryam's mortal remains in the casket welled up her eyes with swirls of tears!

"Here it is!" Nagabhushanam pointed at the showroom as they reached the destination.

CHAPTER 6
A Clue That Eluded a Breakthrough

"He was murdered!" the second-hand vehicle dealer revealed after thirty minutes of pleadings and deliberations.

Suryam leaned against the body of a sedan and said to the dealer, "Sir! Nagabhushanam is innocent! You also know it. Help him come out of this case! He was accused of smuggling fake currency in the Acer van you sold. It so happened that he found Rs.2 lakhs in that van before he abandoned it. That Rs. 2 lakh was fake currency! You alone know the fact that Nagabhushanam bought it from you and on your advice, he abandoned it! Please advise the owner's details who asked you to put the van on sale! That fellow will know the background of this fake currency!"

The reluctant dealer sheepishly asked, "Fake currency in the van?"

"Yes!" Nagabhushanam replied.

The dealer said once more, "He was murdered!"

All the three looked at the dealer wide eyed.

The dealer said nervously, "Leave this place immediately. Nagabhushanam's photo is being telecast on the TV that he is eluding the police!"

The three were shocked at the news!

"Why did you ask Nagabhushanam to abandon the van?" Suryam questioned.

The dealer continued, "I bought the van from him for Rs. 2 lakhs. I paid him one lakh in advance. Later, he visited me seeking the balance amount. I asked him for documents. He said he didn't have any documents and that was why, he said, he sold it for such a low price. We had an argument. He left cursing me. Later, I learnt that he was murdered.

"At that time, I sent my man and returned your three lakhs and advised you to abandon the vehicle!"

"Any more information? Anyone else came enquiring about the van? Suryam pleaded with the dealer.

"Yah! Last month a man by name Veeraiah met me. He also enquired about the van's owner! Recently, I saw in the newspaper that Veeraiah died in a road accident. I'm sure it's not a road accident!"

"Veeraiah! He was a retired Havildar! He was our senior. I went to his funeral at Bhadrachalam," Suryam was shocked to discover that his uncle's death might not be due to a road accident!

"Yes. I remember he told me he is a retired army staff," the dealer said.

Kirtana also read about Veeraiah's death in the paper. She knew Madhavi. She met her quite a number of times when the latter visited Suryam's place. She sent a condolence message to Madhavi and her mother.

"Why do you think it may not be a road accident!" Suryam questioned.

"Leave this place. I've entertained you because I thought I should clear your doubt as to why I returned you three lakh rupees and why I asked you to abandon the vehicle!" The dealer hastened them to leave the stockyard!

"Don't you have the contact number of any family member of the Acer van owner?" Suryam implored.

"Why do you need it?" the dealer asked.

"It will help to fix the case!"

"His son used to threaten me that he would lodge a complaint to the police alleging that I planned his father's murder; he tried to blackmail me. I didn't care about him. He demanded that I return the vehicle or money! Once in a while he will contact and abuse! Lately, I blocked his number! Last month, he came to the showroom and made a big fuss!" the dealer said.

"How much do you owe him," Suryam asked.

"Because I didn't return the van to him, one can say, I owe him one lakh. But I lost four lakhs in total because of his father's irresponsible dealing."

"We will pay him one lakh! Meeting him is important to know more about his father! Two honest soldiers were accused and were arrested. A dedicated soldier who died fighting with the Maoists was also accused. Please share his contact number," Suryam requested.

The dealer thought for a while, and shared the number! He said, "Don't ever try to contact me!"

The three had come out of the second-hand vehicles' stockyard. It was late in the night. The three decided that they would rest in a hotel room and would meet the son the next day!

* * *

It was 2 a.m. Ravindra reached the Hotel Taj, a star hotel, the location registered by GPS. He walked up to the reception. He told the names of Kirtana and Nagabhushanam and asked whether they checked in. "Two rooms were booked for three occupants!" the reception staff confirmed. Ravindra realised Suryam travelled along with Kirtana and Nagabhushanam.

Ravindra showed his visiting card to the hotel staff and requested to connect him to Nagabhushanam. The hotel staff declined to disturb their guests at that hour!

Ravindra booked a room. He obtained the room numbers of Kirtana and Nagabhushanam. He checked in and dialled them through the intercom. None responded. He was frustrated. He walked up to the rooms and knocked on the doors. None responded. He reported the matter to the hotel staff. The staff had no choice but to examine the issue and they found there was not a guest in those two rooms!

* * *

Next day at 7 a.m. The constable at the Paloncha police station reported to the CI. "Sir! Good morning! Major Ravindra's location is showing Hotel Taj, Banjara Hills."

* * *

8 a.m. Ravindra received an incoming call from Nagabhushanam!

Nagabhushanam got access to his phone only when Kirtana and Suryam left the hotel to meet the son of Acer van owner. They stayed in Hotel Minerva.

Ravindra landed at Hotel Minerva as quickly as he could upon learning that Nagabhushanam was at the hotel. Nagabhushanam apprised in detail and said to Ravindra that Sardar was very intelligent and helpful! At the mention of the title 'Sardar', Ravindra understood Suryam had not disclosed his identity.

Ravindra was impressed by Suryam's decision to book rooms at two different hotels simultaneously. While booking at the Taj Hotel, Kirtana accessed her phone and paid through Phone Pay. As a result, the GPS tracker showed Ravindra their location as Taj Hotel. At Hotel Minerva a debit card was used and the phones were put in power off mode.

"Why have you not accompanied Kirtana and Sardar?" Ravindra enquired Nagabhushanam.

"My photo is being telecast on the TV," Nagabhushanam explained. He divulged the entire discussion they had with the second-hand dealer.

"Give me the contact number of the son!"

"I don't know," Nagabhushanam sheepishly said. Ravindra was filled with intense anger and frustration. The fresh set of news of the murder of the Acer van owner and the road accident involving Veeraiah had his head spinning with disbelief and outrage.

He thought he should immediately stop Suryam from probing the case further!

He sent a WhatsApp message to Kirtana from her dad's phone: "Please call me, it's urgent!" Only one tick mark appeared.

He turned to Nagabhushanam and said, "Uncle! It's not safe for you to stay here. The police may arrive. Let's leave!"

"That's why I contacted you. I feel safe now!" Nagabhushanam displayed his amiability and affection to Ravindra and followed him!

* * *

"The dealer wants to settle your one lakh. Let me know your address!" Suryam told the son of the man who was murdered.

"Use Phone Pay!" a curt reply came. Suryam was ready with an answer. "We have cash only!" The son reluctantly gave his address.

When Kirtana and Suryam reached the address located in a slum, they saw a one room shanty; a sick woman was lying half-consciously in the shabby bed. The weight of poverty could be felt. Suryam contacted the son once more!

'Hand the cash to my mother. Give the phone to her!"

Suryam handed one lakh rupees and Kirtana's phone to his sick mother. She confirmed to her son that she received the cash! Her son disconnected the call immediately after.

Suryam tried his number and it was not reachable. He demanded his mother to return the cash. She secured the cash under a thin pale mattress, slept over it with legs flayed and clasped it tight with her hands. Suryam argued with her; she screeched for help and neighbourly women gathered. "Tell me where your son is?" Suryam yelled. A woman replied, "He is not in Hyderabad!" Suryam and

Kirtana were shocked. They enquired the neighbours about the background and the details of the murdered man! All the women dispersed! A few well-built men had arrived, and they had a uniform answer for any question: "We don't know anything. Leave the place!" It had become nearly impracticable for the two to stay there any longer. Suryam gazed at the shanty and found the sick woman was missing! He walked up to the bed and lifted the stained and lumpy mattress. There was no cash!

Suryam and Kirtana dejectedly got into the SUV and drove back. Suryam was driving inattentively and became disoriented. Something else captured his imagination. As he was leaving the shanty, he saw a calendar on the wall. It was torn and discoloured. There was nothing on the page of the calendar except a photo of mushrooms wrapped in plastic boxes! No other detail was evident. When Suryam enquired the neighbours about the calendar, no response was received.

Suryam was driving without knowing where to go. He racked his brains, pushing himself to remember something that had slipped his mind. "Mushrooms?" He read or saw or heard about mushrooms somewhere. He intensely tried to recollect, digging deep into his memory. No use!

Kirtana too realised they hit a cul-de-sac. They lost money. A crucial lead that they had hoped would be valuable turned out to be fruitless. All hope was lost.

She contacted her father. She thought it was good to have an update on his safety!

She heard Ravindra's voice!

"Kirtana! You dad is safe with me. Police are behind us to arrest him. I have clinching proof to show that he is not guilty. You only have to give in writing to the police along with the evidence and also file for an anticipatory bail. I cannot do that. I'm part of the investigation. I myself should not validate that your father is innocent. It's time you leave Sardar and return. Where is Sardar?"

Her blood simmered. She spoke to her dad and understood that her father and Ravindra were in Ravindra's SUV! Her father also requested her to return. She disconnected the call and powered it off! That short time was sufficient for Ravindra's GPS to register her location!

Kirtana was agitated. She was more worried about proving Suryam's innocence. Proof was eluding her and Sardar! She resolved she would not leave Sardar as long as he was pursuing the investigation. In case he left, she decided she would fight it alone!

Suryam asked her, "How is your dad!"

She sarcastically replied, "He is SAFE with Ravindra! Your boss is special and he nailed it. I guess we may wind up and go back!" Unaware that the statement from her was made at an inappropriate time, she failed to realise how Suryam had misinterpreted her. The true intent of her words was lost on her, and she was oblivious to the confusion they had caused.

'He is safe with Ravindra. Your boss is special and he nailed it! We may wind up and go back??' Her words echoed. Suryam was annoyed. He felt she was looking for the right moment to bid goodbye to him.

He recalled an incident. Her father said, *"Sardar says his boss has sent the police to arrest me. Why will Ravindra get me arrested when......"* At that moment, he observed her using a stern gaze to quiet her father. 'What was it that she didn't want me to know about which her father inadvertently almost let out!' he wondered.

Uneasy silence reigned.

Suryam thought he was losing hope on all counts. He was not able to recollect the context of 'mushrooms. He sensed Kirtana was gratified that her father was absolved of accusation and Ravindra cracked it! He was bothered that she trusted Ravindra! 'Who was concerned about the innocence of Suryam? Who was worried about two soldiers who were jailed?' he reflected.

He resolved to pursue the case no matter what happens.

Suryam braked the vehicle at a side. He looked at Kirtana and said, "Ma'am, we are not able to make a breakthrough! I believe it may take longer."

Kirtana didn't answer. She was at a loss for words. She felt like saying. "Sardar, we shall jointly continue the probe!" But she remained incoherent.

She was pleading inside, "God! Show me a way! I don't want Sardar to abdicate the mission!"

Both stepped out of the SUV and stood on the footpath.

Suryam said, "Good bye, ma'am! Not sure whether we will meet again!" His voice suffocated.

"So, what next?" she asked, muffling the tremble in her voice.

"I'm not sure. What about you? What next?" he enquired, accepting leaving her as an inevitability. He yearned to say, *"Kirtana, there are no words that can fully express how much you mean to me. You are the light that guides me. You are the strength that sustains me. I don't know where I'd be without you, and I can't imagine ever being without you again. Please, always remember how much I love you."* But he could not express.

"I will pursue the probe till my last breath! Suryam is innocent! I don't mind if I die in the process," she wanted to say! She could not shake the feeling that she needed something more to say to him. She believed she should say that! She cleared her throat and when she was about to say it, her attention was grabbed by a lady whom she knew well! Suryam too looked in that direction. His eyebrows raised with surprise.

He saw Madhavi and her mother walking along the footpath. Suryam walked briskly toward them. Kirtana saw Sardar wishing Madhavi and her mother. She followed him, absolutely surprised how Sardar had known Madhavi!

Madhavi's mother greeted Kirtana. She informed her daughter, "Kirtana is here!" She gaped at Sardar and said she was not able to recognise who he was! Suryam said that Havildar Veeraiah was his colleague and mentor and lied that he attended the funeral of Veeraiah!

Kirtana learnt that Madhavi had an appointment for an eye surgery. She noticed they were standing opposite LV Prasad Eye Institute! She herself was a doctor! Madhavi asked her mother to show the reports to her. A cloth bag was hanging on the shoulder of her mother. Madhavi said, "LV Prasad Eye Institute provides treatment free of cost to the dependents of defence personnel. It's all dad's blessings! If I get sight, I owe it to him!" Suryam was moved. He asked, "I hope you brought the service details and related papers of Veeraiah! The hospital may seek his information!"

"Yes. We submitted dad's service sheet. In case of need, dad's bible is with me! Dad recorded every detail in it!" Madhavi, using her sense of touch, searched for something and pulled out her father's diary from the cloth bag.

Suryam saw the diary! His mind sparked! He jumped like a kid! He remembered he read about the mushrooms in that diary! He involuntarily took it from Madhavi's hands and quickly perused a few pages that Veeraiah wrote before his death. He was thrilled to read the information in the diary!

He felt a surge of excitement. Luck favoured him, he made out. He said to Madhavi, "I've to go urgently! Will meet you quite soon!" He strode forward and with a sudden impulse, he turned on his heel and gazed at Kirtana and said, "Ma'am! Good bye! Wish you all the best!" He spotted an auto and waved his hand. She saw Sardar getting into the auto and departing!

As she watched him depart, a mix of anxiety and surprise surrounded her. *'Where is he going? Why has he left me behind?'* She didn't waste a second. She too bid farewell to Madhavi, got into her SUV and followed the auto!

* * *

"This is the location last registered," Ravindra said pointing at the LV Prasad Eye Institute at his side!

"We've got to keep on moving, uncle! The police by this time would have known that I picked you from the Minerva hotel. They must be tracking us!" he worried.

Nagabhushanam shouted, "That's Kirtana's car! She has turned left!"

CHAPTER 7

Suryam Hit the Bullseye

As Suryam approached the premises of Gold Mushrooms Private Limited, a large mushroom manufacturing unit, he was met with the sight of a towering compound wall. The vast yard, which spanned approximately 50 acres, was enclosed within the confines of the wall, serving as a formidable barrier to any intruders.

With caution, he carefully made his way, taking care to avoid any obstacles or hazards along the way. He found a secluded spot to mount the wall. The sounds of the staff bustling about inside the facility could be heard from afar as they went about their tasks of packaging mushrooms, loading and unloading crates, and attending to other tasks.

Undeterred, he managed to climb the wall, taking care not to get caught. The yard, once he entered it, appeared to stretch on for what seemed like an eternity, and he could see the various chambers and structures that dotted the area, serving as homes to the many different types of mushrooms grown.

As he approached the chambers, he took care to move about silently and stealthily, blending in with his surroundings to avoid being spotted by any of the staff.

As he searched for chamber number ten, his heart raced with excitement and anticipation. He had to find it, no matter the cost.

But as he searched through the open yard, he saw only nine chambers. He sneaked past lumps of dry grass, rows of fermentation chambers, and state-of-the-art mushroom spawning chambers, his eyes scanning the area for any sign of the elusive tenth chamber.

Suddenly, something caught his eye. A bundle of dry grass, untouched by anyone, was ring-fenced and isolated from the rest of the yard. It was as if it were calling out to him, beckoning him to come closer. He carefully crawled on his stomach towards the isolated area. He noticed an obscure spot within the yard which was surrounded with electrified barriers to prevent intruders. No one had access to the cordoned off area.

* * *

"Shall we go left, or right?" a puzzled Ravindra asked Nagabhushanam as they lost track of Kirtana's SUV a couple of minutes before. Nagabhushanam looked at him clueless. He contacted Kirtana and her phone was powered off. As far as he was concerned, the investigation was over! He was pleased that Ravindra had the evidence to prove he was not guilty! His sole desire was that Kirtana should stop going ahead with Sardar and return!

"I guess she has not gone far!" Nagabhushanam guessed.

* * *

Kirtana, driving the car, watched Sardar climbing on one side of the mushroom factory. She reached the factory. She noticed an entrance gate and a security guard. Mini transport vans with loads of packaged mushroom boxes were leaving the factory from the exit gate. Trucks with loads of dry grass straw, manure and sawdust were entering through the entry gate. It was a very well-designed modern mushroom producing unit. She drove around the premises. She saw another entry and exit gate at the far end of the premises. She returned to the parking area.

One hour was over. She was worried about Sardar! All through this time, she introduced herself as a doctor and engaged a word or two with the security guard. She decided to gain entry. She said she'd like to purchase fresh mushrooms at the factory counter! The security guard made note of her details, allowed entry to her and guided her to where she should go!

Suddenly there was the sound of gunshots! There was pandemonium. Workers ran helter-skelter. Transport vans and grass and manure trucks were stranded as the drivers and workers jumped off the vehicles and ran for safety.

Suryam was running with a pistol in his hand. He was running down the mushroom yard toward the entrance gate. He had to run through multiple paths intersecting huge structures, machinery, warehouses, stocking yards, grass yards and transport lorries. He was scampering like a Cheetah. Kirtana noticed that Sardar sneaked into a mushroom spawning chamber. She managed to reach him. He hid behind a rack. He was surprised to see her. He said quietly that he urgently needed army backup. He told her a phone number and asked her to dial it. Even before he completed the number, she said, "This is Ravindra's number! I have it." She felt an urgency to assist him. "You have his number?" he questioned. "Yes! Of course!" she replied as she was in a hurry to dial Ravindra. When there was a response, she said, "Sardar wants to speak to you!"

Suryam moved to a corner and said in a quiet tone, "Sir! I got it! I witnessed bundles of currency in an underground chamber! Please summon our unit to seize the chamber!"

"Where are you?" Ravindra felt elated at listening to the voice of Suryam. He was exhilarated that at the nick of time he was boarding the mission. He heard Kirtana addressing Suryam as 'Sardar'. 'Suryam had not disclosed his identity yet!' Ravindra measured.

"In the premises of Gold Mushrooms!" Suryam replied.

"I'm right outside it. I can see the clamour. You come out!" Ravindra ordered Suryam.

Suryam was shocked. Was Ravindra standing outside the premises? He instantly grasped that Kirtana guided him. He sensed why she preferred to travel with him till then!

It seemed a synergy between Ravindra and Kirtana, he guessed. But why was she doing it, he grappled for an answer.

Two armed guards of the unit were approaching, searching for the man who entered the underground chamber. The Chamber 10!

Kirtana felt she should flee. She looked for Sardar. He had just left and was running ahead of her. She thought she should catch up with him immediately. She had to pass through a spawning chamber which looked like a shortcut to reach him. She stepped inside it to get out of the other end of the exit door. She crossed rack after rack. The steel racks were 15 feet high. It was dark inside. The chamber was getting auto shut. She hit a rack and fell down. She lost her phone. The mechanised doors of the chamber were fully shut and she was groping in total darkness! She banged on the racks and the walls. The walls were thick and she hardly generated any noise. She screamed for help! Frantically, she began to scratch at the floor with both of her hands, desperately searching for her phone, but to no avail.

* * *

Amidst chaos, Suryam spotted Nagabhushanam. He hurried over to him and asked, "Sir, do you happen to see Ravindra?"

"Sardar, he went in to protect Kirtana! He is worried!"

Suryam grew absolutely furious. Ravindra, Suryam expected, should hasten to seize chamber ten. He should summon the army police. He should have positioned himself at the security gate and taken charge of the situation. Unable to stomach the superfluous priority of Ravindra to protect Kirtana, Suryam questioned, "Is there a need to worry about her?"

"Sardar, after all they both have a bond to worry about each other," Nagabhushanam twinkled his eyes seeking Suryam to guess why and when a man and woman would worry about each other!

Suryam was overcome with a sense of disorientation and confusion. Despite having fulfilled the duty of uncovering the mafia case and reporting about it to Ravindra which was what he planned he should do, he felt a profound sense of emptiness and disconnection. He felt lost! He felt he could not stay there for another moment, as if some invisible force was pulling him away from that place.

He said to Nagabhushanam, "Sir! Inform Ravindra…... your…..." He felt reluctance and discomfort to add any further words.

"……..would-be son-in-law!" Nagabhushanam finished it with a bright smile on his face.

Up until that moment, Suryam had assumed that Kirtana was leaning towards collaborating with Ravindra to prevent her father's arrest. It was a distinct reason altogether! His mind went dizzy. He grasped that Ravindra was right. Ravindra said a woman would love to marry a wealthy man. Kirtana preferred Ravindra. She had only shown compassion to him, Suryam reasoned. He admitted that he lost the bet.

"Sir! Inform your son-in-law that I lost the bet with him," Suryam said dejectedly and left the place. Nagabhushanam didn't see Sardar so desolate! He muttered to himself, "What bet?"

Ravindra in fact took immediate action by notifying the army police and urgently summoned their presence at the factory. He was ecstatic. It was happening the way he envisaged.

He entered the office building of the factory to take control and not let key promoters' escape. He was eager to call for a press conference and announce the unravelling of the scam. He was also searching frantically for Suryam! A brief update and a formal investigation report from Suryam were immediately required.

* * *

TV news channels were telecasting breaking news: "Good evening, we have breaking news. A massive scam involving fake currency worth more than hundred crore has been unearthed in the premises of Gold Mushrooms Pvt Ltd. The scam was brought to light by Major Ravindra, who discovered the fake currency in underground chambers during a raid. The modus operandi of this massive operation involved the movement of counterfeit money through porous international borders in the north east and south west regions of the country. Shockingly, the promoters have confessed to the crime, and within minutes of their confession, Major Gururaj committed suicide. The promoters mentioned his name in their confession, claiming that they had his support in this illegal operation. As the investigation progressed, a separate transport smuggling network was traced, and the promoters were taken into custody by the army police. We have Major Ravindra with us at the crime site. Mr Ravindra, please share the story with our viewers," the news anchor presented the mic to Ravindra.

Ravindra was on cloud nine. He briefed, "After an extensive investigation, we were able to uncover a major fake currency racket. The investigation led me to an underground chamber at this unit where we found fake currency worth crores. The suspicion that an unscrupulous officer connived led the army to pursue the investigation. The promoters of the unit eventually confessed to the crime, but it was unfortunate that the promoters claimed the support of an army officer. Major

Gururaj who committed suicide had connived with the promoters as confessed by them. Gururaj knew an investigation by the army was on the cards to uncover the Hyderabad mafia. He planned to shift the epicentre of the investigation from Hyderabad to a remote mofussil location. He selected three soldiers from Paloncha town and dispatched envelopes with fake currency to their camp addresses. His plan almost worked for him. Luckily, I didn't fall prey to his plan but dug into the case till I nabbed the real criminal. I'm happy I've done it. The crime initially led to the wrongful incrimination of three dedicated soldiers. Two of them who were under arrest will be released. Another soldier, Mr. Suryam, who died in a Maoist attack, was also not guilty. I am grateful to all the members of my unit who worked tirelessly to ensure the success of this operation."

Kirtana was eventually rescued by the army. She fumbled through the darkness and upon emerging out of the chambers, she was stunned to witness Ravindra confidently addressing the TV channel in a live telecast, claiming credit for unravelling the crime.

With a newfound sense of resolution, Kirtana strode vigorously towards her SUV and drove off with focused intent. Ravindra remained oblivious, engrossed in conversation with the anchor while Nagabhushanam watched him with admiration, completely unaware of Kirtana's departure.

* * *

Two hours before-

Nagabhushanam realised Ravindra was searching for Sardar. He said to him that Sardar had left dejectedly a while ago and asked him to inform that he lost the bet with Ravindra! "What bet is it?" Nagabhushanam even enquired Ravindra.

"Before departing, what was the last thing he mentioned? Do you know where he is headed?" Ravindra questioned in an acutely frustrated voice.

"He merely stated, *"Inform your son-in-law that I lost the bet!"* That's all. He walked away hanging his head in desolation!" Nagabhushanam replied, unable to understand what was bugging Ravindra so much about Sardar!

"Why didn't you stop him?" Ravindra shouted.

Nagabhushanam had put up a perplexed face not able to fathom as to why he should stop Sardar from going anywhere! His only worry was about his missing daughter!

Ravindra showed Sardar's photo to two of his soldiers and commanded them to search for Sardar. The soldiers returned after one hour and informed Ravindra that they found Sardar's headgear and Ray-ban glasses beside a rail track. He was stunned. He silently prayed that Suryam had not taken his own life. 'Who will submit the investigation report except Suryam?' He felt nervous. He believed that he had no other recourse but to speak to the media and assert that he had successfully uncovered the mafia.

CHAPTER 8

Love Conquered All

Valet parking staff followed her. She rushed out of her SUV and galloped. The security guard saw her sprinting like a deer bypassing the metal detector door and he pursued her to ascertain who she was. She enquired a room number as she crossed the reception. The reception staff craned their necks and watched curiously as the valet parking staff and the hotel security guard followed her. She took to climbing the stairs avoiding the elevators. Her mind was deliriously agog. The palpitations of her heart were fluttering and skipping a normal function. She felt a nervous shiver filled with excitement and thrill. Her index finger quivered as she pressed the calling bell.

Suryam opened the door and was stranded in disbelief to see Kirtana. Kirtana laid eyes on him in what seemed like an eternity, her eyes welled with tears. She had heard that he was no more, but here he was, standing right in front of her, alive in blood and spirit. She wrapped her arms around him, squeezing him as tightly as she possibly could. Tears streamed down her face as she wailed uncontrollably, her relief and joy impossible to contain.

When Kirtana had come and held him in a tight embrace, an indescribable surge of joy and love filled him.

"Who told you I'm here?" he asked shockingly as he passed her car keys to the hotel staff.

"Let me come inside," she felt at home as she made her way by gently pushing him aside, stepped into the room, closed the door, gazed at him anxiously and questioned, "Rishil, what happened? Why did you put on Sardar makeup?"

Suryam ordered coffee before he recounted to her his experience of surviving a Maoist attack at the Indravati river. He narrated how Ravindra instructed him to go undercover and join his mission to capture the culprits. He went on to share that he refused to move in disguise because he believed Kirtana wouldn't be able to handle the news of his demise. He said Ravindra poked fun at love and their relationship. He told her how he countered his boss and warned him not to ridicule his relationship with Kirtana. He showed a copy of the bet agreement to her.

Kirtana read it and burst into laughter! She came near him and said apologetically, "I'm sorry. The rules of the agreement made me laugh. But I'm thrilled to know you undertook an unusual risk to prove a point about our relationship."

She hugged him and said, "Rishil, I recognised you at the mushroom unit that you are my Rishil! Your makeup, accent and tone didn't fail you. Guess how I could identify you?"

"Maybe my headgear went off."

"No. Your makeup is intact!"

"I don't know!"

She wearily asked, "Rishil, why didn't you care to rescue me. I was stuck in a chamber at the mushroom unit."

Suryam looked puzzled. He explained that he felt lost when he heard about the marriage alliance between her and Ravindra. "Who said it?" she questioned.

"None other than your dad!"

"I'm sad you trusted my dad and jumped to a conclusion!" she posed a straight rejoinder and it caught him off guard. He lowered his head in a gesture of shame, guilt and embarrassment.

Tense mood set in. She picked the diary on the table and with an intention to divert the topic and ease his mood, she asked, "What is in this diary? How did it help you?"

"It's my uncle's diary. I flipped through it inattentively when I attended his funeral. I read words like 'chamber 10', 'gold mushrooms pvt ltd'. Those words faded from my memory till I observed the pictures of mushrooms on the calendar at the shanty. I struggled to recall where I had previously read about mushrooms. I unexpectedly met Madhavi and noticed the diary in her possession.

"What important thing did he write?" she grew inquisitive.

"He wrote that he saw a network of currency smugglers across the international border of India and Bangladesh. Poor women were deployed to carry fake currency in crumpled cloth bags. A woman would walk all the way to a designated spot and deliver the unnoticeable wrinkled cloth bag to another impoverished woman. She invariably would carry a months old kid to fake it better. The second woman would walk and deliver the bag to another woman in the next town. The chain goes on. This network had nodal hubs across the country. The bags would be delivered from place to place unnoticed. Hyderabad was a major hub. My uncle, after retirement, happened to see, in Hyderabad, a woman with a kid tugged to her waist and a soiled cloth bag hanging on her shoulder. It aroused suspicion in him. He trailed her. She delivered the bag to a man who was driving a mini transport van. The van was driven to Gold Mushrooms Pvt Ltd. After intense detection, my uncle found an underground chamber where fake currency was stacked. He named it chamber 10. There were nine chambers visible to the naked eye."

"Super!" Kirtana screamed gleefully.

"Uncle wrote that a van driver, who was part of the racket, rebelled against the promoters and was murdered. I understand the van driver was the same guy who tried to sell the van to the second-hand dealer. My uncle intensified his spying on the factory and it was clear now that he was also murdered. It was portrayed as a road accident."

"Oh! My God," Kirtana felt sad.

"Who told you that I checked into this hotel? Have you met Madhavi's mother?" he asked her.

"Yes. I guessed you would reach the eye hospital to support Madhavi. I met your aunt at the hospital. My guess was right. She said you had put up in this hotel. She and Madhavi were thrilled to know that you are alive."

"Yes, Kirtana! We are doubly happy that Madhavi's eye surgery is successful. She will be discharged tomorrow!" a relaxed Suryam stated.

"Many times, it occurred to me that you could possibly be my Rishil, but I was not entirely sure. Your makeup, accent and tone never failed you. Your bodily gestures, your unconscious habits hinted a lot. Every time I thought I should confront you, the casket allegedly carrying the mortal remains and lying in the mortuary held me back. What is in the casket?" she asked with a broad smile on her face.

"I don't know. Ravindra managed it."

"Time is up," Kirtana smilingly asked, "By now, you should guess how I recognised you?"

"I'm hands up! I'm unable to guess," he surrendered.

She showed him a photo on her phone!

As she showed him the photo on her phone, he saw an image of himself and Kirtana. They were facing each other with their backs to the camera, and a tattoo on Kirtana's right shoulder caught his attention. The tattoo depicted a young man kneeling on a dinghy, with his arm extended to receive something, while the name 'Kirtana' was written alongside the image. Similarly, he noticed a tattoo on his own left shoulder, which portrayed a young woman standing on the same dinghy, offering a lotus flower, with the name 'Rishil' inscribed below.

He understood that when they stood together with their shoulders exposed, the tattoos created a complete image of a man receiving a lotus flower from a woman on a dinghy.

"Rishil! I never dreamt that the tattoos and the photos we took in Gokarna would one day prove to be so invaluable!"

"It was the same image I drew with charcoal in the house at the riverbed, our meeting spot! I'm still trying to grasp how the tattoo helped you?" he voiced his confusion.

"At the mushroom unit, I happened to notice that the left shoulder of your shirt was torn exposing the tattoo. I was thrilled. I tried to catch you while you were running away. I was then stuck in the chamber," she clarified. As he reminisced, he remembered the feeling of his shirt snagging on the barbed wire as he crawled through it.

"When is Ravindra proposed to you?" he enquired.

"It was a few weeks ago. I believe it was prior to the date of your betting agreement with him. My dad was hellbent convincing me to marry him. I rejected him," she answered with a hint of annoyance in her tone.

Suryam's face lit up with pleasure as he learnt Kirtana rejected Ravindra upfront.

"Where are Sardar headgear, Ray-ban glasses, wig and beard?" she asked as a playful glint appeared in her eyes.

"I threw them away while I was returning on the MMTS train," he laughed.

In a teasing tone, she asked him, "On a lighter note, tell me who emerged the winner in the bet between you and Ravindra!"

"It's ME ONLY! I discovered the underground chamber. I uncovered the mafia. And my conviction that you will never forget me has just been proved right!"

"Who will let Ravindra know that you are the winner? He was celebrating by holding press conferences and publicising that he unearthed the mafia." She gave him a quizzical look as she posed him a question. She switched on the TV and news channels were telecasting the breaking news and Ravindra was seen giving interviews.

Suryam said furiously, "Right now, I will announce that I'm alive. He will be doomed." He was about to dash out of the room.

Kirtana held him. She said, "I fixed Ravindra," and she explained to him what she did!

* * *

An hour ago-

"Ravindra, congratulations!" cheered Lt Col. Ravindra stood in attention and saluted the Lt. Colonel at the Cantonment Military Corps Office. He heard a sense of disparagement in the Colonel's tone. The Colonel fixed him with a sharp, scrutinising gaze, as if attempting to delve deep into the character and personality of his subordinate. Ravindra attempted to smile and ease himself but felt disconcerted.

The Colonel pressed the buzzer and an office staff came in. He nodded to the staff to send someone inside. Ravindra was stunned to see Kirtana entering the office room of the Colonel from the antechamber. Kirtana thanked the Colonel for his time. She was offered a chair and was made to sit comfortably.

"Ravindra, where is Suryam?" "Who is Sardar?" The questions were posed by the Colonel in a direct and succinct manner, similar to the way an arrow was shot at its proximate target. Ravindra was shaken. The floor beneath his feet quaked.

"Whose body parts are lying in the casket in the government mortuary alleged to be the mortal remains of Suryam?" the Colonel thrusted a spear. Ravindra's face turned gaunt and pale.

"What led you to suspect that Gold Mushroom's premises had fake currency in the underground chambers?" the Colonel thumped on the table.

"And finally, can you give me your investigation report right now?" the Colonel yelled.

Ravindra had no answers. He was stupefied. *'How the Colonel gained knowledge of the events that transpired between me and Suryam?'* his body convulsed uncontrollably as a wave of fear and anxiety washed over him, taking complete hold of his senses.

The Colonel angrily stared at Ravindra and said, "Kirtana raised these questions and you need to answer!" and he threw a written complaint paper signed by Kirtana on Ravindra's face!

"Ravindra! She said to me she saw Suryam. Is he alive? I want a straight answer?" the Colonel thundered. He recalled his soldiers finding a Sardar headgear and Ray-ban glasses beside a rail track! He sheepishly said, "His headgear is found at the rail track!" His voice trembled.

"The Circle Inspector of Police contacted me. He expressed dissatisfaction with the fact that you were accompanying one Mr. Nagabhushanam, while at the same time requesting the Inspector to search for him and arrest him. What is this drama?" the Colonel roared ruthlessly. Ravindra could not open his mouth.

"Your silence does not help you, Ravindra!" the Colonel hollered. There was no reply from Ravindra except a frozen gaze at the long walls of the Cantonment building designed in the colonial era.

The Colonel commanded in a steely voice, "Ravindra, you are suspended. I order an inquiry."

Kirtana turned to Ravindra and said, "Ravindra, you advised me not to squander my life participating in street protests defending a shallow feeling called love. I feel grateful that God has made the experience of love comprehensible to only a select few, and I am humbled to be among that chosen few." As she was leaving the office room, she passed by Ravindra and showed him a photo on her phone, mentioning that the photo had helped her to identify Suryam who was in disguise as Sardar.

Ravindra wished he confessed to her, "Kirtana, not only you but Suryam is also among the select few chosen by God. Suryam believed that your love for him was pristine! He is right. He won the bet. Good luck!"

He watched Kirtana marching victoriously out of the Cantonment office. She resembled an embodiment of the spirit of LOVE who loved Suryam so endearingly, stood by the tribulations of the challenge with conviction and won her cause and lit the victory flame merrily.

THE END